The Red Dress

Gaby Halberstam lived in South Africa until the age of fifteen, when she and her family moved to Britain. She began writing stories at the age of five. Gaby studied English at university, and although she went on to qualify as a lawyer, she knew from the first day that she would rather be writing. She now lives in London with her husband and three children. *The Red Dress* is her second novel.

Praise for *Blue Sky Freedom*

Shortlisted for the Waterstone's Children's Book Prize 2008

'An engrossing story set in 1970s South Africa . . . an impressive debut' *Scotsman*

'Halberstam's writing is both sensitive and exciting' *Telegraph*

'Important and powerful' *Carousel*

D1004477

Also by Gaby Halberstam

Blue Sky Freedom

The Red Dress

Gaby Halberstam

MACMILLAN CHILDREN'S BOOKS

First published 2009 by Macmillan Children's Books
a division of Macmillan Publishers Limited
20 New Wharf Road, London N1 9RR
Basingstoke and Oxford
Associated companies throughout the world
www.panmacmillan.com

ISBN 978-0-330-45053-9

1 3 5 7 9 8 6 4 2

A CIP catalogue record for this book is available from
the British Library.

Typeset by Intype Libra Limited
Printed and bound in the UK by CPI Mackays, Chatham ME5 8TD

Acknowledgements

Thank you, as ever, Lucy, for your warmth, encouragement and support. Thank you Melanie, Sharon, Sophie, Julie and Moira for your enduring patience and attention to detail. A deeply felt thank-you to Harriet Wilson, without whose trust I would never have begun this book. Thank you also to Emma Young, and all the team at Macmillan.

Mom, without all your memories and your inimitable spirit and humour, where would I be? And, above all, Simon, Sophia, Noah and Boaz – thank you for everything.

In memory of my father, Harold, 1930–2008

For Shirley, my mother, and for Hilda, my aunt

Part One

Part One

Chapter One

Johannesburg, South Africa. January, 1944

Outside on the platform, the stationmaster blew his whistle once. Rifke Lubetkin smiled. She loved its shrill, rolling sound. It marked the beginning of their holiday. Already the train was snorting and hissing, straining to move. The warm evening breeze blew smoke past the window. One more minute and they'd be off.

The porter pushed the last suitcase under the seat and stood in front of them. He took his cap off. Sweat trickled down his face. Their luggage had been heavy.

'Madam,' he said. He shook his cap a little. Rifke's mother bent to check the suitcases. Maybe she hadn't understood what he wanted. Nineteen years in South Africa, and Ma could barely manage more than a few stunted sentences in English. Yiddish was the language she'd brought with her from Lithuania, and it was the language she continued to speak. None of Rifke's friends' parents were still so foreign.

She tapped her mother on the back.

'Ma! Hurry up. The porter wants a tip,' she said in Yiddish.

'*Ya*, Rifke, *ya!*' She eased herself upright, scowling.

The stationmaster blew the whistle twice. The porter shifted from one foot to the other.

3

'Hurry, Ma!' Rifke said.

Muttering under her breath, her mother pulled her purse out of her handbag and began to scrabble in it.

The train jerked and clanked.

'Ma! The train's going!'

Rifke leaned over her mother. She put out her hand to help poke out a few pennies.

'*Nayn!*' Her mother whipped round and slapped Rifke's fingers. The sound rang out in the small compartment. Rifke gasped and flapped her hand. How could she do that to her? And in front of a stranger too. She'd be fifteen in three weeks and five days, yet Ma treated her like she was five. She sat down with a thud on the seat and pressed her hot face and smarting hand to the cool glass of the window. She heard the scrape of the pennies, heard them drop with a tinny clatter into the porter's hand and heard his mumbled thank you. He left the compartment. Through her tears she saw him again, back on the platform, tilting his cap backwards and wiping his forehead.

Doors were slammed and the train began to clang and grind and hiss. Slowly, majestically, it shunted through the station. Rifke took a shuddering breath. At long last. The beginning of a week of freedom from the everyday grind – even if it was with Ma. It was 7.20 p.m. now. Almost an hour past their usual bedtime. She wiped her nose on her sleeve and tossed her head. Just let Ma try to make her go to bed at 6.30 when they got to Kimberley.

She watched the lights and trolleys and people slipping past as the train picked up speed. Soon the darkness of the backdrop made a mirror of the train window, and Rifke was able to look into her own eyes. Their grey-green didn't show up well, but the lights inside the compartment cast an interesting shadow which accentuated her high cheekbones. She could be the heroine in a film. Tossing her two tight plaits, she threw her shoulders back and lengthened her neck. A young Deanna Durbin leaving her old, miserable existence for a life of luxury with her newly discovered father. Of course she would be desperately sad to leave her old friends, and her job cleaning out the pigsties in the mansion of the evil Madame Dufour. Rifke squeezed out an extra tear. But what could she do? She shrugged with what she thought looked like resignation. Her mysterious and drippingly rich father had summoned her. She had to obey his call.

'Rifke!' Her mother's high wail came from near Rifke's feet. What did she want now? Rifke folded her arms. Ma could jolly well sort it out for herself. She tried to get back to her daydream. Where was she? Oh, yes – her father's call.

'My medicine case! Rifke – it's not here.' Her mother was on her knees, some of the suitcases dragged out from under the seat.

Damn that medicine case.

'Rifke! Stop the train!' she shouted.

Rifke ripped herself away from the telegram her

5

fantasy father had sent. She looked over her shoulder. Ma's mouth was stretched into a rectangle. She was scrabbling to stand, pushing hard against Rifke's knees. Before Rifke could stop her, she'd clambered on to the seat and was reaching for the emergency cord.

Rifke grabbed her mother's sleeve. 'Ma – Ma! You can't just pull the emergency cord! Your medicine case is on the rack.'

She leaped up next to her mother and pulled aside the raincoat the porter had slung there. She yanked the little tan leather case out by its handle and handed it to her mother.

'Here.'

Imagine if she hadn't been able to stop her! Rifke felt a blush crawl up her neck. Thank goodness no one else had seen. Rifke jumped off the seat and sat down again.

'*Got tsu danken!*' Ma fluttered her hand against her chest, then grabbed the case and set it on her lap. She unlocked it with the smallest key on her bunch and opened it. It gave off a strange smell – a mixture of leather and sour chemicals.

The case was small, but it was crammed. Ma always said the *Malech-hamovess*, the Angel of Death, was never very far away. Sometimes Rifke thought he lived next door, the way her mother carried on. The Angel of Death had a servant, the Angel of *Krankeyt*, or Sickness. Ma's medicine case contained all her ammunition to knock him out before the Angel of Death could get a look in.

Rifke knew the contents off by heart. For the head, there were Grandpa's Headache Powders and aspirins. For the throat – blackcurrant pastilles in a decorated tin and cough mixture. For the skin – a new bar of Palmolive soap and Pond's cream. For the back – a piece of red flannel and some mustard to make a poultice.

But far more important than any of these was the stuff for the bowels, for *oysmachen*, as Ma so delicately put it. Apart from Eno's Fruit Salts and Milk of Magnesia, there was a bottle of Chrysmol for Rifke. Clear, colourless refined liquid paraffin that made her stomach twist and churn like a trapped eel. For her mother, a bell jar, filled with solid minced-up dried fruit that Rifke thought looked exactly like . . . like *kak*. Rifke blushed again with the thrill and shame of just thinking the word. It was this jar that Ma had been looking for. She took it out, together with a dessertspoon wrapped in a hanky, and placed them on the small fold-out table.

Rifke had already had her dose of poison at home. She watched her mother scoop out and swallow a spoonful of her secret weapon against constipation, and then, after a second's thought, another. She replaced the jar in the case and gave it to Rifke to put back on the rack.

Rifke wedged the case into a corner. Why did Ma insist on bringing it with them to Kimberley? And her own soap too. Aunty Leah and Uncle Ber and Mirele hardly lived in the *bundu*, the wilds of South Africa. And

7

while they weren't millionaires, they weren't exactly poor either.

Warm smells of roasted meat and gravy drifted from the dining car into the compartment. Rifke listened to the clatter of plates. She and Ma had had their dinner at five o'clock. Her tummy rumbled. Ma looked up and tutted. She'd read Rifke's mind.

'*Gebrotn khazerl . . . treyf*,' she said, frowning. Roast suckling pig . . . definitely not kosher: anything not kosher was roast suckling pig to Ma. She rummaged in her handbag and brought out an apple. 'Eat, eat my child,' she said to Rifke, rolling it around on her out-stretched palm.

The rules were tight and strict. They could eat only certain animals, and then only if killed and prepared in a certain way. Dinner on the train was forbidden. Being Jewish wasn't easy, Rifke thought as she took the apple.

Thanks to Aunty, who'd sent them an extra ten shillings specially, they had the compartment to themselves. Rifke turned off the light. While her mother muttered her prayers, Rifke lay on the top bunk trying to work up her daydream again.

Chapter Two

The tall man had his back to her. He was wearing a hat. An overcoat was draped over his wide shoulders, and a streamer of smoke curled from the cigarette in his hand.

'Dad!' she called.

The man began to turn.

'Rifke. Rifke.'

She felt her arm being shaken. 'It's six o'clock. Get up now, it's time.' Ma flung back the bed linen and snapped the light on. Rifke blinked, confused. The rumble of the wheels beneath them and the swaying of the compartment reminded her they were still on the train. She burrowed her head into the pillow. Five more minutes and she would have seen her father's face.

Rifke's mother thumped the mattress twice. 'In one hour and twenty minutes we will be there.' She pushed a stack of folded clothes towards Rifke. Rifke groaned.

Ten minutes later she was sitting on the seat in the cotton dress Ma had packed for her. Rifke hoped Mirele wouldn't recognize it. When Mirele had grown out of it, Aunty had sent it to Rifke. It had come in the box with the food she sent every month. For three years it had hung, together with all the other cast-offs, drooping on its hanger, waiting for Rifke to grow into it. Even now it

9

was loose around the waist and far too long. Something was scratchy on the inside of the dress in the left armpit. Rifke squirmed on the seat, raking at her skin.

'I must do your hair is a mess. Be still.' Ma was sitting behind her, unravelling Rifke's night-time plaits. 'Rifke, Rifke, what are you sitting on – *shpilkes*?'

'Yes, exactly. I'm sure there still are pins and needles in this horrible dress.' Rifke tugged her head away from the teeth of Ma's comb. 'Ow! You're hurting me, Ma. I can do my own hair.'

'*Sha, sha,*' Ma said, but she drew the comb through Rifke's hair more gently this time, and the light touch Rifke felt on top of her head might have been a kiss.

Soon they were sitting side by side on the leather seat. Rifke's long mousy hair was tightly plaited and looped up with green ribbons over her ears; her mother's streaky hennaed hair was in a roll at the base of her neck, netted up and secured with black metal hairpins. The pins made Ma's head look like it had been badly stitched together. Rifke scowled and scratched at her armpit again. One hour to go.

She pulled up the blinds. The sky was banded in orange and lilac. Rifke leaned her forehead against the window. When her breath misted the glass, she wrote 'Princess Rifke' and the date on it. Behind her, Ma was powdering her face and rouging her cheeks. The chalky sweet smell made Rifke sneeze. She heard the plippy noises Ma always made when she put on her lipstick, and

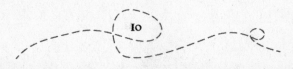

she knew without looking that there'd be little clots of 'Femme Fatale' around the edge of her mouth. There was silence for a moment, then came the muttering of prayers.

Half an hour to go.

'Do you think Mirele will have grown even taller?' Rifke asked.

When her mother didn't reply, Rifke turned around. 'Ma?'

Ma was sitting bolt upright, and Rifke could see she was tightening up. Her mouth looked like it had been pulled by an invisible drawstring into a tiny pucker, taking all the Femme Fatale with it. Her fingers were laced and twisted into a clench, the joints white. Rifke sighed. Why did Ma always have to be like this when they went to Kimberley? She turned back to the window.

The train was beginning to slow. They were passing farms, the light catching the corrugated roofs of the dotted-about farmhouses, the small, beige scribbles of sheep. Rifke pulled the window down and leaned out.

'Rifke –' Ma gasped. 'Be careful!'

Bunching a handful of Rifke's dress in her left fist and gripping the sill with her right, she too leaned out of the window. Rifke took a deep breath. Gusts of warm air and smoke brought the dry, sandy smell of earth and burnt soot straight into her nose and made her plaits flap. Even Ma was enjoying it. Rifke could hear her sniffing deeply. The train tooted three times and huffed out a billow of steam while, under their feet, its tendons were tensing. Rifke looked down the brown flanks of the carriages.

'Ma! I can see the station!' Rifke laughed.

She leaned out a tiny bit further. All the way down the train, heads were blooming at the windows. 'I can see Uncle Ber and Aunty and Mirele!' She just had time to yell, 'Mirele!' before Ma yanked her back into the compartment and pulled the window closed.

'Behave yourself. That is *grob* behaviour, Rifke.' Ma pulled Rifke round and held her face between her palms. 'I must clean your face is dirty.'

Rifke pulled back, but Ma's spit-moistened hanky got there first. Then her plaits were tugged and the ribbons crisped and her dress tweaked and her socks twitched. 'OK now,' Ma grunted.

Rifke decided not to say anything about the huge soot smut next to Ma's left eye. Serve her right, she thought, and a giggle fizzed up inside her.

The train had slowed right down. It drew level with the beginning of the station and sighed as it nosed its way alongside the platform.

'They're there! I saw them. We passed them, Ma.' Rifke pressed her face to the glass. Aunty had seen her. She was scuttling down the platform towards them, with Rifke's sister, Mirele, loping at her side.

The train stopped. Rifke hurled herself down the steps and flung herself into Aunty's open arms.

'Rifkele, Rifkele.' Aunty staggered a little. She

squeezed Rifke against her pillowy bosom and kissed her forehead twice. But when Aunty pressed her cheek to Rifke's, Rifke felt Ma grip her arm tightly and make a noise something like a growl, and Aunty moved away quickly.

'Ma –' Rifke frowned.

But Ma had moved towards Mirele, who was standing apart. A loop of her normally sleek dark hair stuck out above her ear.

'Mirele,' Ma said, reaching out a hand. Rifke knew she wanted to smooth it down, but just at that moment Mirele ducked away and leaped to Rifke's side. Out of the corner of her eye Rifke saw Ma's hand hovering in space for a few seconds.

Mirele bent over Rifke and gave her a peck. 'Hello again, Rifke. I heard you shout.' She grinned and flipped one of Rifke's plaits before leaning over to kiss Ma's cheek. Ma swung her head away and the kiss landed in Ma's hairnet. Mirele caught Rifke's eye and shrugged.

Mirele lived with Aunty Leah and Uncle Ber. Ma had been too poor to look after both sisters. So before Rifke could properly remember any different, Aunty and Uncle had been bringing Mirele up as the daughter they'd never had.

Rifke looked up at her sister. She hadn't seen her for about six months. Damn! She was even taller. Now it'd be four years before Mirele's clothes would fit her. But on the other hand – Rifke found her sister's height interesting. Ma was tiny; so was Aunty Leah. Mirele was a giant. So it must have come from their father.

Rifke watched as Ma allowed Aunty to hug her, hands fisted at her sides. Yet again Ma had brought all her grudges with her to Kimberley; they must have been tightly packed in her medicine case along with all her other ammunition. Why did she have to be so difficult? Rifke frowned and kicked at a loose stone. Uncle Ber would say something funny and make it better. She looked around for him.

'Uncle Ber has gone to the car with the porter,' Aunty said. 'Come, come, Toiba, Rifke. You must be hungry, tired.'

Rifke ran towards the car park. She could see Uncle Ber's grey-blue Chrysler gleaming at the end of the row. She felt a surge of pride. Uncle Ber was leaning against the bonnet, smoking, his suit jacket straining from the middle button. His hat was clapped on to the back of his head. The morning breeze carried the smell of his cigar towards Rifke. He gave an exaggerated start when he saw her.

'Is this really you? *Shaineh maidel* – a girl as beautiful as the seven worlds,' he said, throwing up his hands.

'No, Uncle!' He always teased her. 'Stop it.' She gave him a mock smack, then dashed over to the back of the car to greet George, Uncle Ber's black driver. He was packing their suitcases into the boot.

George drove extra slowly through the quiet Kimber-

ley streets. The houses were low-lying; all the buildings were. Even John Orr's, the department store, was only two storeys high. Kimberley's pavements were gravelled, not paved, and people said sometimes you could find semi-precious stones or even diamonds twinkling among the pebbles. Rifke never had, even though she always walked with her head down and her eyes unblinking.

The car swished on. Rifke wished Veronica Stapleton and Betty Williams, the rich girls in her class, could see her now. She sat up straight and raised her chin. She was Princess Elizabeth waving through the window of her carriage.

'Did you see someone you knew?' Mirele asked.

'What? N-no. I was just, er . . .' Damn. Mirele must have been watching her. She felt suddenly hot, squashed up by Ma against the car door, and her left armpit began to itch and prickle again.

Aunty and Uncle's house was a comfortable home among others just like it, in an avenue lined with pepper trees. As George steered the car home, Rifke looked out of the window at the servants scrubbing the *stoeps*, or polishing cars, or watering gardens. There were few white people around at this time of the morning.

'Oh, Aunty, you've painted the house.' Rifke flung open the car door as soon as George braked in the drive. 'Wow – it looks just like a house in a magazine.' The front garden was full of billowing plants, twinkling with water droplets. Rifke stood for a moment in front of the gate.

Everything was bright and dazzling to her eyes – the fresh yellow paint on the walls of the house, the white iron lacework, gardenias in the flower beds and pink and red roses in barrels on either side of the path.

There was a commotion coming from the car. Just as Rifke turned to see what was going on, Ma came clopping towards her at top speed, a look of panic and concentration on her face. She bustled past Rifke and headed straight through the open front door.

'Ma . . . ?'

'*Oysmachen*,' Aunty said, coming up behind Rifke.

Bowel movement. Rifke covered her face with her hands. How could Ma embarrass her like this? And it *was* embarrassing, even if they were among family. Aunty put her arm around Rifke and patted her twice. 'Come. Come. I have a surprise for you. And then we will have breakfast.'

Chapter Three

Aunty took Rifke's hand. She led her into the house and down the passage. She stopped in front of the French windows that led outside. 'Look!' she whispered. Her dark eyes were shining.

Rifke peered through the glass panes at the back garden. It was a big square, mostly grass, with apple and pear trees laid out in a grid towards the end. Behind the trees was a fence with a small gate, which led to a tennis court owned by the people who lived next door. Dappled with soft sunlight, and peaceful, nothing looked different.

'What, Aunty? I can't see anything.'

'There. Under the tree.' She pointed at the huge, ancient kaffirboom to the side of the garden.

Asleep in the shadows at the base of the tree was a big black animal. Rifke pressed her nose to the glass and blinked.

'A dog? Where did it come from? Whose is it?' She turned towards Aunty. 'It's not yours, is it?'

'Yes, yes, Rifke.' Aunty nodded. 'One of Ber's customers asked him to take it. She couldn't look after it.' Aunty put her hand on the door handle. 'We will go see.'

Rifke hadn't been very close to a dog before. Or not

willingly. There was a horrible dog in the park that always jumped up and raked its muddy paws down her uniform, and Mrs Tunkel's Minnie who yapped and bared her needle-teeth.

As soon as the dog heard the door opening, it leaped up and bounded towards them. It hurled itself at their feet and rolled on to its back, its tongue unravelling from its mouth like a long, sodden rag. Rifke hung back and sheltered behind Aunty.

Mirele came up behind them. She threw herself on to the ground and let the beast nudge and paw at her and wipe her face with that floppy, bubbling tongue. Rifke peered around Aunty's back. Ma would go berserk if she saw that. Lots and lots of wriggling germs, and all of them completely non-kosher.

'Stroke him, Rifke.' Mirele got to her knees and offered Rifke one of the dog's paws. Rifke took a step backwards and gripped Aunty's arm more tightly. 'What? You're not scared of Atticus, are you?'

Usually Mirele was friendly. She understood what Rifke had to put up with, living with Ma. At least she said she did. But last time Rifke had visited, Mirele had been a bit impatient with her. And now she had a scornful look on her face.

'Of course I'm not scared,' Rifke lied. She let go of Aunty and stepped slowly towards the dog. She put out a forefinger, which trembled a little as it hovered six inches away from the animal.

18

'Oh, for goodness sake, Rifke.' Mirele wrinkled her nose. 'Honestly – it's not as if he's a lion or anything!'

Rifke took a deep breath. She had to do something, and quickly, before Mirele moved off. She flung herself to the ground. Atticus pressed his snotty nose to Rifke's. He stank of fish and mud and a hint of something else that might have been *kak*. Rifke squinched up her eyes. She was running out of breath. She sniffed, gagged, swallowed the sour bile.

'*Feh!* Disgusting!' From nowhere Ma had appeared. 'You fool!' she shrieked. 'The animal is dirty – disgusting dirty germs he will give you!'

Rifke opened her eyes to Ma's thick ankles and her best brown lace-ups. Ma grabbed her arm and dragged her across the lawn. Her bottom bounced against the ground as Atticus barked and scampered along beside them.

'Stop it, Ma!' Rifke yelled. She tried to wrest her arm free and fend off Atticus at the same time.

'Toiba!' Aunty shouted at Ma. 'Leave the girl. She is fine.' She ran over and put her arm out to calm Ma.

Ma swung her free hand at her sister and the dog. 'Go away!' Her face was puce and bunched up. She shook Rifke. 'Get up.'

Rifke got to her feet. She rubbed her arm and her backside. Mirele came over and grabbed Atticus by his collar. Ma all the while was muttering and shaking her head. She blamed Aunty, and Rifke was sorry about that.

Mirele grinned and gave Rifke a rub on the back. 'See – I told you he wouldn't bite. More than I can say about Ma though,' she added in a whisper.

Rifke smiled. She was bruised and muddy and she stank of dog and her mouth tasted revolting. But it was worth it. Mirele didn't look so scornful now.

Ma watched over her as Rifke scoured her face with Palmolive and scalding water and brushed her teeth three times. And what a relief it was to get out of the scratchy dress and into the white blouse and skirt Mirele had passed on to her when they'd last visited.

'Take this to the *shikse* can wash it.' Ma held out the dirty dress.

'She's called Farieda!' Why couldn't she refer to the maid by her name? And why did she always have to join the end of one sentence to the beginning of the next? There wasn't a lifetime limit on the number of words each person could use.

Scowling, Rifke grabbed the dress and ran down the passage. Syrupy, warm smells drifted from behind the kitchen door. Pots were being bashed together, a sign that Farieda was angry with Alfred, Aunty and Uncle's butler-gardener-handyman. Rifke pressed her ear to the kitchen door.

Farieda was the coloured woman who cooked and cleaned for Aunty and Uncle. She'd worked in the homes of just about every nationality, picking up, like a magpie, the secrets of their special recipes. Aunty had taught her

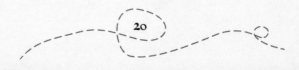

to make the eastern European delicacies Uncle Ber – and Rifke – loved. Many of Kimberley's finest Jewish ladies drooled over Farieda's crispy but gooey *taiglach*, and her fluffy *kneidels* at Passover. In her quiet way, Aunty boasted that Mrs Lipschitz, *the* Mrs Lipschitz, of the Grand Hotel Lipschitzes, had even tried to poach Farieda.

But even though Farieda had been with Aunty as long as Rifke could remember, there was always an air of uncertainty about her. You never knew when she might just fly away, taking her recipes with her.

'You too slow! Make more quick, Farieda,' Alfred said. 'Master and Madam, and our visitors, they are waiting for their breakfasts.'

Alfred came from Nyasaland – a country that seemed so faraway and magical to Rifke. One of her earliest memories was touching his beautiful, shiny brown face.

'Put your teeth back in your mouth, old man,' Farieda shouted. Her voice sounded like newspaper being torn. She clashed some more pots together.

Rifke smiled. Everything was just the same as ever, even down to Alfred's loose false teeth, which clattered when he spoke. Rifke opened the door and stepped into the sweet warmth of the kitchen. Sunlight beamed through the big windows and through Aunty's collection of red Bristol glass on the windowsill. It cast a pink glow on Farieda's tightly wrapped yellow headscarf, on

Alfred's starched white apron and on the black-and-white chequerboard linoleum floor.

'It's good to be back!' Rifke said.

Alfred swung round, his face split into a four-layered smile.

'Little Rifke. Welcome.' He took the brass tray out from under his right arm and bowed. He always made her feel important.

'Who does he think he is?' Farieda clicked her tongue against her palate. She placed a soapy hand on Rifke's shoulder. 'Hmm. You've grown a *bietjie*, but I'm still taller than you,' she cackled. 'Now what's that you hiding behind your back?'

She took the dress from Rifke and held it up. 'Bladdy dog.' She snorted, and poked at her hair under her head-scarf with the back of a wooden spoon. 'Do you think I've got nothing better to do than to make clean after you? You too big now to be rolling yourself on the ground with a dog, my girl.' Tucking the dress under her arm, her mouth curled into a gummy smile. 'Hoo, Rifke – there is some very nice boys now staying there by the tennis-court neighbours.' She jabbed Rifke in the ribs with the spoon. 'Very, very handsome English boys. Twins. One for you and one for your sister.'

Rifke felt the blush creep from the base of her neck and slowly up her face, filling her ears on its way up her forehead and into her hair. She turned away, hoping Farieda wouldn't notice.

'Heh, heh!' Farieda cackled again. 'You looks like you is needing a bit of cool air. Why don't you go tell Madam and Master and Mirele and Mrs Lubetkin breakfast is on the table?' She turned away from Rifke to slot the toast into the ribs of the toast rack. 'And what you doing, old man?' She twisted her neck to glare at Alfred. 'Grinning there like a bladdy *bobbejaan*. Quick, quick. Do some work around here, baboon.'

Rifke felt sad as Alfred pushed his teeth into his mouth and closed off his smile. She patted his arm as she left the kitchen to call everyone to the table.

Chapter Four

Later that day, lunch over, Rifke wandered on to the veranda that ran around the front of the house. Everyone was out there. The sun had been blazing all day, but it was now beginning to tire. Uncle Ber put his newspaper down and, dragging over a rattan chair, he set it down between Mirele and Ma.

'Sit yourself, Rifkele,' he said, patting the worn cushion in the middle of the seat.

Aunty was pretending she wasn't dozing, but Rifke could see the whites of her eyes as she kept nodding off. Next to her, Mirele had pulled her knees up to her chin and was looking at a magazine. Rifke knew from Ma's darting glances over her knitting that she would have loved to say something to Mirele about her unladylike posture or, better still, to give her bony legs a smart slap. Rifke shuffled about in her chair, and the creaks it made joined the unrelenting chirp of the crickets in the bushes, the rattle of Aunty's snores and the click of Ma's needles. Now and then the dog barked from the back garden.

Alfred brought out a tray of homemade lemonade and set it down on the rickety table in front of them. Rifke helped herself to a glass. She held it in her best languid, Hollywood manner, admiring the elegance of her turned wrist, before allowing herself a discreet sip. She could get used to this lifestyle. Cocktails in the late afternoon, a hint of the beautiful sunset to come. Her father in the background, clinking ice in his glass of gin . . .

She looked across at Mirele. There was so much she wanted to ask her. Ma always pulled her mouth into that tight pucker whenever Rifke asked her anything about her father. Aunty and Uncle always exchanged a glance and went quiet. Rifke had tried Mirele many times before. Perhaps now she would tell her something.

Every time the crunch of the gravelly pavement announced the arrival of passers-by, Mirele gave Aunty a sharp poke with her elbow. Startled, Aunty opened her eyes extra wide and sat up straight. Uncle Ber tucked his newspaper into the side of his chair and Mirele put her feet on to the floor. It was like a little mechanical scene and it made Rifke laugh. Whoever it was out for their late-afternoon stroll would stop in front of the gate, some just to say hello, others to tell Aunty and Uncle some bad news, usually about the war in Europe.

At first Rifke listened to their conversations, smiling when they noticed her. But it soon became boring, and she stopped paying attention. Ma, on the other hand, looked as though she was really enjoying herself. Rifke watched her nodding and smiling as sunlight flashed off the octagonal lenses of her glasses. All in all, Ma hadn't been too bad since that morning. She hadn't muttered at all about the lunch Farieda had cooked. She hadn't even made Rifke wear that stupid straw hat like she had last time.

Rifke closed her eyes.

'Ow!' She felt a sharp pain in her shin. 'Ow!' she said again. Mirele's pointed toes with their long nails were jabbing at her.

'Wake up, Rifke,' Mirele hissed. She jerked her chin towards the garden gate. 'Look who's coming.'

Rifke rubbed her eyes. Two boys were walking up the path. Twins of about Mirele's age. Both wearing white shirts and flannels and striped blazers. They were red-haired, their pale skin sprayed with zillions of freckles. Rifke smiled. *Their* mother hadn't made them scrub their faces with Metamorphosa cream.

'Hello, James. Hello, Alexander,' Aunty said. 'Would you like a glass of orange juice, a glass of lemonade?'

'Good afternoon.' They spoke together, including Ma and Rifke in their polite nods. 'Hello, Miriam.' They grinned.

Miriam? For a moment Rifke wondered who they meant.

'Hello.' Mirele waved lazily. 'Would you like to sit down?'

Of course. Mirele. She never thought of her as Miriam. It made her seem older. And she was so relaxed with these boys. Rifke wished she could be like that.

'Yes. Sit, sit.' Aunty beckoned. 'Chairs, we need chairs, Ber.'

'No, thank you. We won't stay.'

But Uncle Ber had already shuffled over to the corner of the veranda, and was pulling a couple of chairs off the stack. One of the boys went over and put his hand on Uncle Ber's arm. 'We won't sit, thank you, sir.'

Rifke loved their English accents. They sounded just like the newscaster on the wireless.

'We were just wondering if Miriam might like to join us in a game of tennis before it gets dark.'

The other boy was looking at Rifke. Rifke flushed a little and lowered her eyes. She sensed Ma staring at these friendly boys, taking them in, from their slightly grubby canvas shoes to the shorn curls on the top of their heads.

'Oh, sorry. I didn't introduce you. This is my sister, Rifke.' Mirele stood up and stretched. 'I'd love a game of tennis. I'll just go and change.'

'Oh, Rif . . . er, Riffler.' The boy couldn't quite manage her name. He smiled at her, and Rifke smiled back. 'You're already in your tennis kit. Why don't you come now? Miriam can join us on the court.'

Rifke looked down. Even though it wasn't a tennis outfit, she *was* wearing white. Farieda was right – the boys were really nice. And Rifke loved tennis. She put her book on the table and, pressing her hands on the arms of the chair, she stood up.

With a force so violent that Rifke's head was flung

backwards, Ma grabbed Rifke's wrist and yanked her down. She landed in her chair with a thud.

'*Nayn!*' Ma's voice was loud and gruff, and it sounded even louder in the silence that filled the veranda and the garden and the whole of Kimberley. 'Rifke will not play tennis. With boys.' Ma jerked her head once and added, not quite under her breath, 'And not with *goyim*.'

Goyim – everyone knew that meant 'non-Jews'. Uncle Ber drew breath sharply.

Aunty put out a hand as if to ward off anything else Ma might do or say.

The two boys looked at each other, then looked up at the sky, into the garden, out at the street. One of them shifted from one foot to the other, his canvas shoes squeaking on the tiled floor. 'Um . . .' he said.

Rifke shrank into her chair, trying to shrivel herself into something tiny. A scrap of paper perhaps. Let the wind carry her away with one light gust. She kept her eyes down. Tears were banked up behind her eyelids. Mustn't. Must not cry. Out of the corner of her eye, Rifke looked at Ma's hand still tightly gripping her wrist. Sweat trickled from Rifke's armpits and down her sides. She needed to slow her breathing. In – one, two. Out – one, two. Calm, calm, she told herself.

'We, er . . . we'd better go then,' one of the boys said. And the canvas shoes shuffled over to the veranda steps. Ma's grip slackened a little.

'No, no! Don't go!' Aunty and Uncle exclaimed at the

28

same time and pushed back their chairs. Just then Mirele arrived.

'Come on, chaps!' she said, swinging her racket. 'See you later, everyone.' Rifke heard Ma make one of those low growly noises.

Mirele paused at the gate and looked over her shoulder. 'Rifke? Aren't you coming?'

Rifke shook her head and looked down. She waited until the front gate had clicked shut behind them. Then she dug Ma's fingers off her wrist.

'Let go of me!' she shouted, and ran inside, heading for the guest bathroom at the back of the house.

Slamming the door, she ground the key in the lock. The mirror on the front of the medicine cabinet flashed her mottled face back at her. Rifke dashed her tears away with the back of her arm. Ma was not going to make her cry. All the same, the tears sprang up again, blurring the flowery pattern on the curtains. Rifke sank to the floor.

What was Ma's problem? They were really nice boys – polite, quietly spoken. What more could Ma ask for? They'd only wanted a game of tennis, not Rifke's hand in marriage, for goodness sake. And thinking about it again, she drummed her heels on the lino and roared through gritted teeth.

She stood up to look in the mirror again. Great – she looked even more dreadful than before. Stringy hair escaping from the ribbons, glued by tears into clumps. Her thin face patchy, except around her eyes, which were lost and red and puffed up. Who'd be stupid or blind enough to want to marry her anyway? And for a moment she saw herself aged about seventy, all lumpy and saggy, sitting in front of Ma, who was plaiting Rifke's lank, grey locks and looping them into faded green ribbons. She gave a snort that was a mixture of laughter and misery, and a worm of snot shot out of her nose. And that made her look even worse. She yanked her hair free of its ties and after scrabbling it into the worst mess she could make, she subsided on to the floor again.

Rifke didn't know how long she sat there. She only realized she'd been listening to the pock of tennis balls out on the court when the sounds stopped completely. Through the bathroom wall she could hear the muffled pips of the news from London. 'Soviet offensives on the Ukrainian front continue . . .' Rifke knew Ma and Uncle and Aunty would be hunched over the wireless, anxious to hear even the tiniest scrap about what was happening in Lithuania. Ma and Aunty had left two brothers there when they'd sailed for South Africa.

Rifke sat there for a while longer. When her limbs began to feel cramped, she got up and unlocked the door. Ma was standing outside the bathroom about to rattle the handle.

'Rifke! Six thirty. Time for sleep now.' And she reached out to do something with Rifke's hair.

No way was Rifke going to bed then. Jerking up her shoulder, she pushed past, feeling the give of Ma's plump

arm under her hand. Ma made a little scrabbling movement and a small sound.

Rifke stormed down the passage and out into the garden. The shadows at the base of the tree separated and Atticus bounded towards her. He leaped at her side once or twice, but she almost didn't notice him. Lifting her arms, she ran across the garden. Through the trees and along the side of the empty tennis court. Then back through the trees, weaving in and around them until her legs gave way and she fell on her knees. Her breath burned in her throat as she gulped the cool dusk air.

Rifke looked up. The cloudless sky looked bigger, wider than ever. It was violet. Stars glinted. When she was younger, Rifke had believed the night was a huge piece of silk, and the stars were little rips where the light of heaven shone through. She knew better now, but she still liked the idea of a vast tent sheltering every single person in the world. Maybe, thousands of miles away, her two lost uncles in Lithuania were looking up at their piece of sky. Maybe her father too. Was he looking up at the sky, or was he *in* the sky with Ma's all-seeing, all-knowing God, looking down at her. Rifke shivered.

If he was, what could he see? Who was she? Who was Rifke Lubetkin, and what was she in the world for?

Chapter Five

The gate to the tennis court creaked. Atticus leaped up and barked, giving Rifke a jolt. 'Who's there?'

'Is that you, Rifke? What are you doing out here in the dark?' Mirele appeared, looking ghostly in her tennis whites. She stood above Rifke, knocking her tennis racket against her legs. 'We had such fun! Why didn't you come with us?'

'Didn't those boys tell you?' Her voice thick and hoarse, Rifke told Mirele what had happened.

'What? She didn't? How embarrassing! No wonder they didn't say anything. Oh my goodness, I'm never going to be able to face them again.'

Then Mirele leaned over her and put a hand on her shoulder. 'Poor little Rifke,' she said.

Pity? That was the last thing Rifke wanted. She pulled away from her sister's touch. Mirele took a step backwards. Silence hung between them for a moment.

'I'm going in now.' Mirele tugged her cardigan around her shoulders. 'Maybe you should too.' Tucking her racket under one arm, she made for the house. She was halfway across the grass when she stopped. 'You know, Rifke, you could try standing up to her a bit more.' She

moved off again. Rifke watched her go. The light came on just as Mirele reached the French windows.

'Aunty says come inside.' Mirele's voice rang out across the lawn. 'Farieda left some dinner out for you.'

Rifke stood up and followed her sister. She patted Atticus before going in. Aunty was there. She locked the door behind Rifke. 'Come, come. You must eat,' she said, drawing Rifke towards the kitchen.

Out of nowhere, Ma loomed up, her hair in lank plaits over her shoulder and her old, grey dressing gown tied tightly under her big bosom. It made her look like an overfilled sack about to spill. She frowned at Rifke, her mouth tight, and pointed to their bedroom.

What were Mirele's words? Try standing up to her more, she'd said. Rifke took a deep breath and drew her spine straighter.

'Don't think I'm going to bed now just because you want me to,' she said to Ma, her tone spiky. She felt a tremble begin in her knees. She'd never spoken in that way to Ma before. Even though the tremor was working its way up her body, she managed a defiant smile.

Ma would have grabbed her, had Aunty not stepped in front of Rifke and shielded her.

'Toiba, Toiba,' Aunty said, her soft voice smoothing and caressing. 'Let her eat first. It is a long time from lunch.' She pulled Rifke to her side and, with her arm around her, guided her into the kitchen. Rifke didn't look at Ma.

When Rifke came into their room sometime later, she could see by a sliver of moonlight that Ma was heaped up under her blankets.

'Good,' muttered Rifke.

She pushed Ma's jar of fruit mixture into a corner and covered it with a sock. On the night table beside her bed Ma's teeth grinned at her from inside a glass, a sediment of the mixture at the bottom. Heady with rebelliousness, Rifke tipped the Chrysmol Ma had set aside for her into the sink and washed it away in a burst of water.

The freshly starched sheet crackled as Rifke pulled it up to her neck. Six more days of sleeping separately from Ma, away from her bad breath and her cabbagey farts.

Chapter Six

From the second she woke up the next morning, Ma was horrible. She flung aside the bedclothes with a fixed but wild look in her eyes. A double dose of Chrysmol was Rifke's punishment for her behaviour the day before.

At breakfast, Ma was convinced Farieda had used a non-kosher egg.

'There is in this fried egg blood!' she announced after peering at it through her glasses.

She rejected Farieda's second offering for the same reason. Then, when Farieda set the toast rack on the table, Ma said she wouldn't eat any because Farieda's fingers had touched the bread. Rifke caught Mirele's eye, and her sister shook her head in disbelief.

All morning Ma bustled about. 'Too dark in the house,' she said, shuffling outside on to the veranda. 'Too hot out there,' she said, coming back inside.

Uncle Ber twinkled and cajoled. Aunty made soothing sounds. Nothing made any difference.

At noon, Farieda helped Alfred bring the lunch into the dining room. *Gefilte* fish with platters of pickled cucumbers, fresh cucumbers, lettuce and tomatoes. Farieda waited in the doorway with one hand on her hip, casting a wary look at Ma.

Ma took a mouthful of the fish and screwed her face into a twist of disgust. Then, stabbing a piece of lettuce with her fork, she held it up to the light. 'Leah, there is sand, insects, on this lettuce is not clean!' she said. 'Is dirty!'

Farieda clicked her tongue against her palate and marched out of the room.

'But, Ma,' Rifke said, hearing the clash of pots coming from the kitchen. 'That's nonsense, Ma. How can it be dirty? I saw Farieda washing it in that stuff – what's it called? Exactly the way you do it.'

'You mean Condy's Crystals, Rifke. *Ja*, I saw her too,' Mirele added.

Ma folded her arms and jutted her jaw. Rifke turned to Uncle Ber and Aunty, both of whom leaned towards Ma, each trying to calm her, to reassure her that the food was clean and kosher and exactly as it should be.

'Toiba, Toiba,' they said in coaxing tones.

Ma put her hands to her head. '*Kopvaitik*,' she said. Headache. 'To bed I am going to lie down.'

The cutlery on her plate clashed as she pushed it away and got to her feet. Like a huge, overflowing cravat her napkin was still stuffed into the collar of her dress. It crackled as she pulled it out and handed it to Alfred, who was standing by the door, his eyes wide.

Rifke, Mirele, Aunty and Uncle sat in silence, listening to Ma stomping down the passage to the bedroom. As soon as she shut the door, there was a moment's silence

before they all relaxed, their shoulders dropping, and Alfred did something with his false teeth that slackened his jaw.

Aunty placed her warm hand over Rifke's. 'Rifke . . . it's all right. Toiba is . . . well, it is difficult for her. She is . . .' Her voice tailed off and she gave Rifke's hand a couple of pats.

It made Rifke feel better. Aunty shifted in her chair and her stockings rasped as her legs rubbed together. There was another moment's silence, broken when Alfred stepped forward with his tray to clear the table.

Mirele stood up and stretched. 'Well,' she announced, 'I'm going over to Sylvie's house. I'm sorry, Rifke, but we've got to finish our project on Shakespeare.' She bent to kiss first Uncle Ber and then Aunty. 'I'll be back quite late, Aunty, so don't worry.' She tugged one of Rifke's plaits on her way out. 'We'll do something together tomorrow, OK?'

Uncle Ber rolled his napkin into its ring and, yawning, muttered something about some paperwork to finish. He left Rifke and Aunty still sitting at the table. Outside, Atticus gave a couple of barks, and a fly mumbled against the window. Rifke was just wondering how she was going to spend the afternoon when Aunty patted her hand again.

'Well, Rifkele, you and I shall go shopping, yes?'

'Oh, Aunty,' Rifke said. 'Yes, please!' She stood up

and, leaning over Aunty's back, she flung her arms around her neck.

Aunty clasped Rifke's hands to her chest and laughed when Rifke pressed a kiss into her soft fat cheek.

Madame Pelletier, Maison des Modes, looked from the outside like someone's home. Aunty rapped the door with the lily-shaped knocker. A sparrow of a woman appeared – smaller even than Aunty – dressed in a black skirt and crisp white blouse, a perfect red circle on each cheek.

'Madame Pelletier herself,' Aunty whispered in Rifke's ear.

She ushered them into the front room, her tiny shoes pattering behind them on the wooden floor. Dresses lined the walls on either side of the room in colours Rifke had seen only in flower beds. And – Rifke breathed in deeply – it smelt like a garden too: fresh, a mixture of sweet peas and roses and a cool hint of mint.

'For Madame, or Mademoiselle?' Madame Pelletier asked.

Was that a real French accent? Rifke wondered.

Aunty pointed at Rifke, and sat down heavily in the chair Madame Pelletier offered her. Rifke shifted her weight from one foot to the other as Madame Pelletier tap-tapped around her, measuring her up with darting little eyes.

Madame Pelletier put one hand to her chin and rippled her fingers, making her rings spark. Then she

disappeared through a narrow door at the back of the room.

Rifke tiptoed over to a rack of dresses and plucked at the filmy fabric of a skirt. She held it out. 'Oh, this is lovely.'

A beautiful sunset on board an ocean liner, the mew of seagulls, and a breeze ruffling her hair and wafting her skirt around her bare, golden legs.

Madame Pelletier reappeared. She tut-tutted, and Rifke immediately let go of the fabric.

'Too big. Those are for ladies.' She held up her arm, garments draped over it. 'These, Mademoiselle, are for you.' Setting them down one by one on a table, she twitched and tweaked at each one to arrange it perfectly. Pink. Green. Blue. Another blue.

But Rifke had already seen the one she wanted.

'No, no,' she said. 'That one. That one there.' She pointed, her hand fluttering with excitement. The colour was gorgeous. A deep red, peeking tantalizingly out from beneath the stack of pastel colours still draped over Madame's arm.

Madame Pelletier stared at Rifke. She compressed her lips into a pout and continued with her slow revealing of each garment. A white dress, embroidered with white spots. Horrible neckline. Madame took her time fanning out the skirt.

Stop, stop it! Rifke shouted inside her head. I don't want that one. You know I don't.

Another pale pink dress. A mint green with a nasty belt. A yellow-and-blue checked skirt – tablecloth, Rifke thought. Come on, come on.

The red dress was next. Madame gathered it up to float it over the pile on the table.

Then stopped.

Something caught her eye. Settling the red dress over her arm again, she leaned over the checked skirt. Frowned. She reached into a pocket in her blouse and brought out a narrow case embroidered with lilies. Slowly she unclipped the fastening; slowly she drew out a folded-up, gold metal contraption, which, with a flick of her wrist, sprang into a handle with spectacles attached. Rifke stared: what was she doing? Rifke tapped her foot on the floor and looked over at Aunty, who shrugged and made 'wait a minute' gestures with her hand.

Holding the contraption in front of her eyes, Madame Pelletier glared through its lenses and scratched at an almost invisible blemish on the checked cloth. Rifke was ready to grab the red dress off her arm. She fisted her hands to stop herself and squeezed her eyes shut.

'Mademoiselle.' Madame Pelletier's voice was tight.

Rifke opened her eyes to the most beautiful dress she'd ever seen. Madame had spread it over the table, and it was like looking into the crimson depths of a giant poppy. Rifke gasped. She reached to touch its petal-soft fabric and to brush her fingers over the ornamental black buttons down the bodice.

Madame Pelletier held the dress against Rifke. Aunty clapped her hands together.

'Oh, Rifkele. Beautiful. It is for you beautiful,' she said. 'It lights your face. Beautiful with the grey-and-green eyes.'

The dress fitted as though it had been made for Rifke. Aunty did up the tiny hooks and eyes at the back, her breath soft on Rifke's skin, and as soon as she'd finished Rifke leaped from the changing room, breathless with joy. She spun on her toes, and the dress swirled and rippled round her, almost endlessly.

Madame Pelletier smiled, revealing a row of sweet-corn teeth.

'Your daughter is happy with this dress, not so?' she said to Aunty.

Rifke and Aunty looked at each other. Neither of them corrected Madame's mistake.

Madame Pelletier placed sheets of fine tissue paper between the layers of the dress as she folded it. Then she nestled it into a tissue-paper-lined, pink-and-white striped box, with *Maison des Modes* written across it in flowing script. She bound it with a pink silk ribbon and, with a flourish, snipped a 'v' into the ends of the large bow.

'Mademoiselle,' she said, presenting the box to Rifke.

Sitting on the bus back to Aunty and Uncle's house, Rifke hugged the box to her chest. It gave off the delicious fragrance of the shop. So wonderful – a dress that

Mirele hadn't already worn. And not three or four years out of fashion either. She couldn't wait to show Ruthie back at home.

And Ma.

Rifke felt a pang of guilt. She knew Ma would have wanted to come shopping with them. Her stomach curdled with worry.

Chapter Seven

She was right to have been worried.

Ma was still in her bed when Rifke and Aunty returned. She rubbed her eyes and blinked as they came into the room. Rifke wondered if Ma was feeling at all sorry for the way she'd behaved earlier.

'Ma,' Rifke said, holding up the box, 'while you were lying down, Aunty took me shopping. We went to a shop that looked like a house and the owner was a real French lady and we found this beautiful dress.'

Ma grunted, pressing a damp facecloth to her forehead.

'Look, Ma!' Feverishly Rifke untied the bow, drew the dress out of its tissue-paper nest, lifted it out and shook it. Leaves of tissue floated free. 'Isn't it lovely?'

Ma sat up, threw the damp cloth down and swayed forwards in the bed. She said nothing.

'It looks even better on, Ma. Even the French lady said so. Look, I'll show you.'

'Yes, yes, Toiba,' Aunty said, her hands clasped over her chest. 'Beautiful, she looks.'

Rifke pulled off her old clothes and slipped the dress over her head. So silky soft and cool. She darted a glance at Ma. Ma's mouth was set in a straight line. And still she said nothing. Maybe she liked the dress, now that she'd seen Rifke in it.

'Do me up, please, Aunty,' Rifke said, and, lifting her hair, she turned her back towards her.

The high-pitched howl tore the air. Aunty leaped backwards and Rifke bit into the end of her tongue with shock. Suddenly Ma was out of the bed and in front of them, her chest heaving under her nightgown, unformed words spilling from her mouth. Before Rifke could do or say anything, Ma lunged at her and seized the dress by the collar. And in one swift movement she wrenched it, ripping it all the way down the back.

Rifke stared in disbelief as the dress slipped downwards and caught on her elbows. She straightened her arms, and the dress slithered to the floor. Tears blurred her eyes and turned the dress into a blood-red puddle. Her knees gave way and she sank to the floor, gathering the fabric together and burying her face in it. She looked up. I will never forgive her as long as I live, Rifke thought.

It was a moment before she took in properly what was happening in the room.

Aunty was backing away from Ma, who was now moving closer and closer to her, waving her arms.

'You took first my one child. Now you take my other. How dare you? How dare you touch her?' she screamed.

'*Sha, sha*, Toiba,' Aunty said softly, patting the air with her plump little hand.

44

That only made Ma wilder, and she rushed at Aunty, roaring at her in a jumble of Yiddish, and clawing at her.

'Stop it, Ma!' Rifke tried to pull Ma away. 'Aunty wasn't doing wrong. She was just helping me.'

'Helping? Helping herself to my children!' Ma bellowed. She swiped Rifke out of the way, so that she lost her balance and staggered against the door frame.

'Stop it, Ma!'

Ma was now head to head with Aunty, her bosom rising and falling fast, her nostrils huge and her face dark. Aunty stood rigid, her soft brown eyes wide with tears.

And then, as suddenly as she'd sprung at them, Ma slumped. She turned away and shuffled back to her bed, keening like an injured animal.

Rifke couldn't bear it any longer. She ran from the room, hurtling down the passage straight into Farieda's awkward arms. 'Rifke –' Farieda lurched backwards. 'What is it? What goes here on?'

Rifke could only shake her head. She took deep breaths. Her throat was closing with the threat of sobs. Farieda took Rifke's hand in her bony, dry one and led her into the kitchen.

'Sit, my girl,' she said. 'What you holding?' She tugged the dress from Rifke's fist and held it up. 'Hoo!' she said, and Rifke buried her face in her hands.

'Th-throw it away, Farieda. Please.' She never wanted to see it again.

Farieda clicked her tongue against her palate. Rifke

was aware of her standing beside her. She heard the creak of fabric as Farieda retied the knot in her headscarf. After a few moments Farieda's rubber sandals flapped across the floor, and then came the comforting drone of the kettle being filled.

The howling from the bedroom stopped. Thank goodness, Rifke thought, and she took her hands from her face. Her eyes had trouble adjusting to the brightness of the kitchen. The dress had gone.

A hoarse cry came from Ma and Rifke's room.

'Your fault!' Rifke heard her mother say. 'You and Ber – your fault!' A clatter of Yiddish followed. Rifke could make out only a phrase here and there. 'You made me marry him . . . alone, you said, a young woman on the boat . . . Europe to Africa . . . alone you cannot be . . .'

Then came Aunty's voice, soothing. '*Genug* . . . enough . . . Let's end this, Toiba . . .'

But Ma wasn't ending anything. It sounded like she was just beginning. 'A cheat, a liar . . . may God help me . . . a womanizer . . . a *shikker* . . .'

Rifke knew that meant drunkard. She stiffened. Who was Ma moaning about now?

'No,' Ma continued, her voice now a growl, 'my heart said to me. No—' The door to the bedroom was shut, cutting her off.

Rifke took a deep shuddering breath.

'Here you are, my girl,' Farieda said, handing her a glass of sugary lemon tea.

It stung the cut in her tongue and scalded the back of her throat, but Rifke wanted that. Anything to wipe out the memory of the torn red dress and her shame at Ma's behaviour.

Farieda put two more glasses of tea on the table. After a few minutes Aunty appeared, white-faced. Her hand trembled as she tucked some crinkly strands of hair back into her bun. She drank her tea, looking sad and unreachable.

Ma's tea went cold.

There were sounds of activity coming from Rifke and Ma's bedroom. When the door was flung open and heavy footsteps sounded in the passage, Aunty and Rifke looked at each other.

Ma loomed in the doorway. She was dressed in her travelling gear: sturdy brown shoes, stiff felt hat, raincoat over her left arm and handbag clenched in her right hand.

'Rifke, visit the toilet. I have packed the suitcases are ready.'

'But, Toiba—'

Ma turned her back on Aunty. 'Hurry, Rifke. We are going. The train this evening back to Johannesburg we are taking.'

George brought the car to the front. As he loaded the suitcases, Uncle Ber and Aunty stood to one side on the pavement, Ma and Rifke to the other. Ma gripped Rifke's arm. Rifke caught Aunty's eye and pleaded with her silently, but Aunty shook her head, helpless and weighted with sorrow.

'Aunty, can I quickly telephone Sylvie's house?' Rifke asked. 'I want to say goodbye to Mirele.'

Ma murmured in her throat, an echo. '. . . goodbye to Mirele.'

'I have already telephoned to her, Rifkele . . . Toiba.' Aunty looked at her watch and frowned.

George opened the rear door. Ma held the back of Rifke's cardigan as she kissed Uncle Ber and Aunty. Aunty started forward to kiss Ma, but Ma turned away, pushed Rifke into the back of the car and struggled in after her. There was a brief moment when no one moved, as though there were still a possibility on that sunlit afternoon that Rifke and Ma would not leave.

'Mirele is not coming. We must go now,' Ma said. George shut the door, stepped into the driver's seat, pulled his own door to and started the engine. Rifke looked up and down the street, but there was still no sign of Mirele. Ma was breathing heavily.

'*Zei gezunt!* Goodbye! Go well!' Aunty called, fluttering her hand.

Ma wound up the window, the fat of her arms jiggling with the effort, panting as she threw her head back against the seat.

Rifke twisted round in her seat and on to her knees. Framed by the oval rear window, Uncle Ber shrugged

and scratched the back of his head. Aunty blew hundreds of kisses with both of her hands.

'Bye, Uncle Ber! Bye, Aunty! I love you!' She kept on yelling, pulling away from Ma's hand tugging at her dress, trying to stop her from shouting.

When would Rifke see them again? She tried to print on her memory the yellow-and-white house and the roses and Uncle and Aunty standing there in the late-afternoon sunshine. And in her heart she had a tearing feeling. Ma's fault. All of it was Ma's fault. Rifke darted a glance at her – a heaped-up, poisonous frog sitting in the seat.

An evil little thought flickered into life in Rifke's head. She didn't love Ma.

She opened her eyes wide. Had she really thought that? No, wipe it away. It wasn't true. She looked through the car window and up into bright blue sky. Was God able to read people's minds? And did it count if it was just an experimental thought, one that had been quickly erased?

The car kept moving, taking Rifke away from the comfort and love she'd so looked forward to.

'Rifkele,' Ma said. Her voice was soft and a bit plead-ing. Rifke folded her arms on her chest and felt her heart harden. Squashing herself up against the car door so that the cold metal handle pressed into her, she shrank away from Ma's hand reaching for hers. The car shook – pot-holes in the road's surface. In Rifke's mind, it became the juddering of a car crossing the rocky terrain of the veld.

Deanna Durbin was bouncing along on the back seat, looking out of her open window. They were driving down an avenue of pine trees. At the end, Deanna could see a low-built white house surrounded by a veranda. On either side of the house were gigantic kaffirbooms in full bloom. Their bright orange flowers looked like flames. The air was fresh and cool. A tall man stood in the shadows of the veranda, dressed in cream. A wisp of grey smoke rose from his cigarette. Deanna flew out of the car before it had completely stopped.

'Father!' she called. 'At long last I have found you. I have only just discovered you are a famous writer, living the life of a recluse in the bush.' She turned, ducked into the car and dragged something off the back seat.

'Look, Father! I've brought my typewriter. I can type at one hundred and twenty-two words per minute. I will help you. Together we will create your next masterpiece.' Deanna struggled to carry the typewriter towards the steps.

The man in the cream suit moved towards her, his arms outstretched to help her.

'My daughter. How long have I waited for this day! My treasure – at long last!'

Chapter Eight

Their flat, when Ma opened the door, was hot and dark and airless. There was a sharp smell of sour milk. Through the one wall Rifke could hear Glen Miller and his big band starting up on the Leibowitzes' gramophone, but the jaunty beat just made their flat more mournful. Rifke moved to the windows to drag the black-out curtains open. A dusty grey light filtered into the room that was both their entrance hall and sitting room. She looked out. People with lives were striding up and down in the morning sunshine in the street below.

Behind her, Ma was already bustling about, unpacking the suitcases, piling up the few bits of clothing they'd managed to wear in Kimberley.

'The washing I must quickly do. You will take it later, Rifke, to the roof and hang it.'

Rifke ignored her.

'Rifke! Did you hear?' Ma clattered over to her. She'd already put on her house shoes, and her heels slapped at their broken backs. She was buttoning herself into her old green housecoat. The one with the oil splashes down the front that Rifke hoped no one else would ever see.

'Look at me when I talk to you.'

'What?' She slid her eyes across Ma's chin and over

her shoulder. Couldn't she just leave her alone? Wasn't it enough she'd ruined her holiday? Rifke turned and concentrated on the tram clanking down the street below.

Ma was silent. For a minute Rifke thought Ma was going to do something, maybe grab hold of her, or shout, and she gritted her teeth and stiffened her body. Just let her try. But Ma only stood there for a minute, tutted, then pottered off to the kitchen.

Good riddance, Rifke thought. She dug her hands into the pockets of her skirt. She should be having Farieda's pancakes now and going into the garden to play with Atticus, not staring at the traffic. More than a week until school. What would she do? Her best friend Ruthie was in Muizenberg, and her other friends weren't expecting her back for a while.

A few minutes later, Ma's voice came from inside the refrigerator.

'. . . to Kalman's . . . for a polony, no, two polonies, and also to Mrs Kossoff a good chicken we need.' Ma shuffled to the doorway between the kitchen and sitting room. 'Rifke! Did you hear me? I want you to go to Kalman's and Mrs Kossoff. The big blue bag you must take, and money from my purse. After you are back you will hang the washing.'

'And won't that be fun?' Rifke muttered, glowering at her mother's back. She stomped off into the kitchen, yanked the blue bag off the hook on the back of the

kitchen door and snatched Ma's purse out of her handbag.

'Don't think I'm doing this because I want to be helpful,' she said, not loudly enough for Ma to hear. 'I just can't wait to get out of here and away from you.'

Ma was in the bathroom now. Rifke listened to her grunting as she grated the washing against the washboard. Then Rifke dashed over to the corner of the sitting room. She pushed the armchair to one side and levered up the square of parquet that covered her secret storage space. She grabbed the squashed box of Cape to Cairo cigarettes she'd slotted under her diary. She'd found them, about a year before down the back of the sofa, with a flattened box of matches. They were her father's. They couldn't be anyone else's. Ma didn't smoke. There'd been nineteen in the pack when she'd found them and she'd smoked two since then. Well, not smoked really. Lit them and allowed the smoke to billow around her. And coughed herself sick. She was saving them for crisis times. They were all she had of her father. They made her feel close to him, and stronger somehow.

The corners of the beige-and-blue box were broken. Rifke pressed her fingers against them. She paused for a second or two. No doubt about it. This was a crisis, if ever there was one. She snatched up the cigarettes and the matches, flung them into the blue bag and replaced the parquet and armchair.

'I'm going!' she shouted, opening the front door.

'A good chicken you must get, Rifke! A good one. No disease.' Ma bustled into the sitting room. 'Maybe better I go with you.' She started unbuttoning her housecoat.

Rifke had to get out of the flat, had to get away from Ma. 'It's fine, Ma!' She banged the door behind her and made for the steps.

'Look carefully when it is killed. Look inside the carcass!'

Rifke could hear Ma yelling down three flights of stairs.

Kalman's and Mrs Kossoff were in Doornfontein, a good half an hour's walk from the Lubetkins' flat. There was a small public garden on the way. Rifke had smoked the second cigarette on a bench there a month or two before. Now she hesitated at the gate. The park was deserted. She fingered the cigarette box through the canvas of Ma's bag. No, not now. She'd stop on the way back.

Kalman's was the biggest kosher butcher in the area. You could smell the blood two streets away. Rifke joined the queue in front of the counter. At the back of the shop an old man with a pained expression and a smeared apron hovered among the swinging carcasses. His skullcap was like a huge black lid on the top of his head. Up a steep flight of metal stairs, from the window in a tiny office, Mr Kalman watched over his kingdom. Raw flesh had made him rich. Fay, his daughter, was in Rifke's class at school. She flitted about with Veronica and Betty, flinging her

chestnut-coloured hair around and neighing like the horses she kept in her very own stable. Fay never admitted that all the fancy clothes and jewellery and holidays in Mozambique came from dead animals.

I bet *she* doesn't have to go on to the roof to hang out the washing, with nothing to look at except Mrs Leibowitz's droopy bloomers and fraying towels, Rifke thought, counting out the money for the meat she'd bought. I bet *her* mother would never tear a dress off her daughter's back. And she's got a father. She looked up at the office. Even if he is squat and red in the face. The two fat sausages of dried smoked meat Ma had wanted were wrapped in brown paper. Rifke dumped them in the bag.

All the way to Mrs Kossoff's, Rifke thought about Fay's life in the Kalmans' mansion in Houghton. Her imagination carried her away, way beyond the descriptions she'd heard from girls lucky enough to see it with their own eyes: the sumptuous furniture, a vast ballroom with huge, twinkling chandeliers, striped lawns with peacocks.

It made Mrs Kossoff's house seem even more miserable. She kept chickens in her backyard. Why Ma insisted on buying her chickens there, Rifke would never know.

Mrs Kossoff opened the front door.

'Ah. Rifke.'

She never smiled, but she looked extra sour-tempered to see Rifke. That was because Ma was so difficult, sometimes bringing chickens back because of blemishes –

chickens she'd spent an hour choosing and inspecting herself. For a moment Rifke felt protective of Ma, but the memory of the red dress quickly wiped away that feeling.

'Go through.' Mrs Kossoff jerked her chin in the direction of the yard.

Even if Rifke hadn't known where to go, the stink would have led her there. The whole of the cavernous, dark house smelt of chicken – chicken feed, chicken kak and dead chicken.

'Which one you want?' Joseph, the young black boy, asked Rifke.

He was standing in the middle of about twenty chickens clucking and flapping and scratching at his feet. It was his job to catch them and pass them on to the slaughterer, who was sitting, heavy lidded, waiting with a glass of dark tea and his extra sharp knife, along the veranda from Rifke.

'That one.' Rifke pointed at a random chicken. She just wanted the whole thing over with quickly. Any second now and that fluffy brown hen with the white speckles would have its throat slit. She turned away and shut her eyes.

'I didn't know you were squeamish, Rifke.'

Rifke opened one eye. It was Dov Kossoff, Mrs Kossoff's son. He was a bit older than her. She used to see him every Sunday at Hebrew classes, but he hadn't been for a long time. He looked different. She opened her other eye. He'd been a tubby boy, but he was tall now. His

eyes were still that strange light blue with a dark ring, thick lashed; he looked at her from out of the corners, sidelong. Thick and black, his hair stood up straight from his head. A wolf, Rifke thought.

'Hello . . . er, Dov.' Rifke felt heat rise up her collar and creep across her cheeks.

'How very sweet. Your squeamishness, I mean.'

Was he mocking her? Rifke couldn't tell.

'They don't feel anything, you know,' he said, moving out from the doorway.

He stepped in front of Rifke, facing her, and looked over her shoulder. Rifke heard squawks and the frantic beating of wings. She heard the slaughterer set his glass down. She heard the clatter of the knife as he picked it up.

'It's about to happen,' Dov said. 'Let me protect you.'

He circled his arms not quite around Rifke, and without actually touching her. He smelt of something Rifke couldn't identify. It mingled with the metallic smell of blood. After a minute, he put his arms back by his sides and stepped back from her. Rifke felt relieved. And disappointed.

He looked over her shoulder again. 'Joseph is plucking your little chicken now. *Ja*, she's beginning to look a bit nude.' He caught Rifke's eye and grinned.

Rifke looked down. Soft, pale brown feathers fluttered round her feet.

There was a slushy, squelching sound. Rifke knew the

entrails were being pulled out. She blocked her ears so she wouldn't hear the sloppy slap of them landing in the metal bucket. Dov was smiling. His teeth were yellow, but not very. Rifke whipped her hands away from her ears. He would think she was such a baby.

Snip. Snip. Snip.

'Just a little manicure,' he said, as the dead chicken's nails were clipped, 'and she's ready.' He looked down at Rifke, trailing his eyes over her face and down her body.

Please may he not see the half-moons of sweat under her arms.

'Do you want to come to Fay's party?' he asked.

'What?' Rifke couldn't believe her ears. She'd forgotten he was one of Fay Kalman's cousins. 'To Fay's party?' Her voice came out thick, and she could feel her dress sticking to her back.

'She won't mind. It's on Saturday night. Starts early. Six-ish.'

Rifke widened her eyes. It wasn't a proper invitation. Not written down, and not even from Fay herself. *Shabbos* wouldn't be out. She couldn't get there. No way could Dov come to their flat. Ma would burst if she knew boys were invited, and she'd burst even more knowing that a boy had asked her – even though she sort of knew Dov Kossoff. They couldn't afford a present for Fay. And Rifke didn't have anything to wear.

'Yes, I . . . I'd love to,' she said.

'Good,' he said. 'I'll call for you at five thirty.' He took

the wrapped parcel of chicken from Joseph, opened Rifke's bag and dropped it in.

'N-not . . . you can't –' Rifke stammered, but only a dry noise came out of her throat.

'See you on Saturday,' Dov said, and winked at her over his left shoulder as he moved back into the house.

Rifke stood there, stunned. It took her a minute or two to understand that Joseph was waiting for her to pay for the chicken. She rummaged in her bag for the coins and handed them over. In a daze, she walked back through the Kossoffs' house.

When she stepped into the bright midday sunlight it burned her eyes and, despite the heat, she began to shiver. Why? Why had she accepted?

Rifke pulled her cardigan tightly around her body. Her dress was clammy now where the sweat had cooled. Dov would call round. Ma would answer the door and tell him through the crack that Rifke wasn't there. At first he wouldn't understand. He'd insist that Rifke was expecting him, and ask to wait. Through the door he'd see Ma's stained housecoat, and the sofa with its leaking stuffing. Ma wouldn't allow him to come in. She'd shout at him. Ma would shut the door in his face before Rifke could explain. Then he'd tell Fay everything. Fay would tell Veronica and Betty, and they'd all laugh and whisper about her.

Rifke turned on the pavement. She had to go back to the Kossoffs'. She had to stop Dov from coming to the flat. She'd tell him she'd meet him somewhere. Yes, Joubert Park. Outside the hothouse. Yes. That'd be better. But what would she say to Ma? Tell her . . . tell her she was meeting someone from school.

She reached out for the Kossoffs' knocker. But what if Ma insisted on coming with her to the park? What then? Rifke's stomach tightened into a clench. There'd be a horrible scene, and everybody would be watching, and – and –

No.

There would be no secrets, no deceit. She would give it to Ma straight. She was going to that party, whatever Ma said. And she'd make sure she was downstairs, on the pavement outside the flats and waiting for Dov, long before five thirty.

Spinning on her heel, she turned away and strode off, the blue bag pounding the side of her leg. She passed the little park without noticing it and reached their block of flats with no memory of how she'd got there. She stormed up the steps.

Flinging open the front door, she shouted: 'Ma! You can't say no. There's a party on Saturday night, and I'm going!'

Chapter Nine

Ma came out of the kitchen. Her fingers were webbed with sticky bread dough, and her arms were dusted with flour up to her elbows. She pushed her glasses along her nose with the back of one hand. It left a claggy smear on the lenses.

'Eh?' she said, frowning.

Rifke took a deep breath. She was sure Ma had heard the first time. 'Ma – I said there's—'

'*Sha*, Rifke,' Ma said, shaking her head. 'The chicken. Bring let me give a look.' And she bustled back into the kitchen.

'Ma – I'm telling you something!' Rifke didn't want to discuss the chicken. And she certainly didn't want to watch Ma poring over its dead body. Fired up, she strode across the sitting room to the doorway of the kitchen. She wasn't going to let this drop.

Ma stopped kneading the dough for a moment and pointed at the bag of meat. 'Put on the meaty side of kitchen.'

Rifke hid the bag behind her back and held on to the handles with both hands. 'No. First I want to talk about Fay Kalman's party. On Saturday. I'm going.'

Ma did that really irritating thing. She bobbled her

head from side to side and, her mouth turned down, she made little tutting noises. Then she raised her forefinger from the dough and wagged it at Rifke so many times and with such force that bits of dough flew off. '*Nayn*, Rifke. You will not go.' She clapped her hands together once and turned her back on Rifke. 'Bring the meat,' she said.

For a second Rifke remained in the doorway, staring at Ma's back. So that was it? No discussion. No reasons given. Just *nayn*. And there was she, willing to be open and honest with Ma, even though Ma had screamed and shouted at Aunty, and dragged them back early from Kimberley, and torn to shreds the most beautiful dress Rifke had ever owned. Rifke felt anger gathering somewhere in the pit of her stomach; she felt it roll and churn and boil, rising up and taking over her body until she couldn't stand there a moment longer.

'You – you evil witch!' she hurled the words at the back of Ma's head. 'I hate you!' She slung the blue bag over her head and across her body, and ran out of the kitchen, skidding on the threadbare rug in the centre of the sitting room. The front door was still ajar. Rifke tore through it and down the stairs.

She lunged at the doors at the entrance to the flats, and, stumbling a bit as she hit the pavement, she began to run.

At first she ran as though she were being chased. She looked over her shoulder once, even though she knew there was no way in the world Ma could have run down the stairs and kept up with her. She had a sense of people moving out of her way, and streets and buildings and the noise of traffic and hooters streaming past her. Then, as she entered Joubert Park, she lengthened her stride and ran with a feeling of elasticity in her legs. Shouting like that at Ma had unlocked something in her. She felt free. Mirele would be so proud of her.

On she ran. Past all the usual landmarks:the bandstand, the hothouse, the art gallery, the fountain and the big trees. It was only after she'd left the park that she began to slow down, her breath burning in her chest and throat, and a stitch stabbing her side. She stopped when she reached Park Station, Johannesburg's main railway station. Above the hooting and clanking of the cars and trams in the street, Rifke could hear the heavy shunting and hiss of the trains. Trying to catch her breath, she bent and pressed her hands against the stone facade, warm from the day's sun. She leaned more deeply to ease the stitch and was surprised to feel the bag shift against her back; she hadn't sensed it at all while she was running. She smiled to think of the chicken whizzing around the park, travelling further and faster dead than it ever had alive.

A few passers-by glanced at her. A wind had come up. Holding on to their hats with gloved hands, they scurried off. Rifke looked up. The sun was fighting a brave, but losing, battle. Huge purple-grey clouds were massing and advancing. The thunder exploded like cannon fire,

63

and the rain came down suddenly and heavily. Rifke flattened herself against the wall, but thought better of it when water began to gush out of a pipe above her. She ran through a doorway and into the station.

The station was whirling with activity and noise. Rifke had to move quickly to avoid the porters dragging trolleys stacked high with luggage or khaki bags of rolled-up bedding. Everywhere people were bustling, checking their watches, calling out to porters, rushing to platforms. Announcements echoed across the concourse, sometimes drowned out by the gush of steam or shrill whistles coming from the platforms. It was hard to believe it had only been two days since she'd been here with Ma, so excited at the thought of their holiday she'd wanted to jump up and down.

Rifke glanced at the clock above the departures and arrivals board. It was already after four o'clock. Ma would be beginning to worry. She thought again of Ma's wagging finger, and the way she'd just said *nayn*, and clapped her hands as though the subject were closed.

'*Nayn*,' Rifke said out loud. She walked across to a little stall and bought a slab of chocolate and a bottle of lemonade, then went over to sit on a bench. Good. Let Ma worry a bit. Rifke would wait in the station until the rain stopped.

She had been sitting there a while when a girl of about twelve approached.

'Is anyone else sitting here?' she asked, pointing at the

bench. Rifke was sitting in the middle. She shook her head and slid to the end.

'Thank you,' the girl said. She smiled at Rifke.

The girl was dressed for travelling. Her pink dress rustled as she sat down and set her matching pink bag on her lap.

'Jeanette, darling.' A tall woman sheathed in pale green tottered across the floor towards the bench. Her heels made polite tapping noises. She was wearing the most beautiful hat Rifke had ever seen – straw with big red silk roses and green leaves, and little rhinestones that twinkled like morning dew. She perched on the edge of the bench next to her daughter, bringing with her the smell of honeysuckle. 'Daddy will be along with Judy in a minute,' she said. 'He's just organizing the luggage.'

Rifke watched as the woman twitched at the tips of one pale green glove with the other, revealing a long, slim white hand. A diamond ring flashed as she gathered her daughter's loose blonde hair away from her face. 'My angel,' she said softly.

Rifke felt a stab in her heart and tears stung her eyes. She looked away.

'Frank!' the woman called, waving. 'We're over here.'

Rifke watched as a slight man holding the hand of a little girl stopped in the middle of the concourse. He looked around, dodged an elderly couple and the porter carting their luggage, and then hurried over. His suit was crisp, as was his panama hat. The little girl was dressed in an outfit that matched her sister's. The man laid a hand on his older daughter's shoulder and squeezed. She smiled up at him.

'We'd better board the train,' he said. 'It's already at the platform, waiting. The porter should be there with our suitcases.'

The man offered his free hand to his wife, and the four of them walked away, linked like a chain.

'When we get to Kimberley,' the older girl said, skipping a little, 'the first thing I'm going to do is . . .'

Rifke strained to hear what she was saying, but an announcement drowned out the rest of the girl's sentence.

Kimberley.

They were going to Kimberley. In a strange way, it was as though they were her and Mirele and their parents in some parallel story – together, happy and loving. And that the life she should have had was moving away from her, never to be seen again.

A vision of Mirele flitted through her mind, wearing a pink version of the dress Aunty had bought her, diamonds twinkling in her earlobes, and flowers threaded through her shiny hair. Ma doesn't love me as much as Mirele, Rifke thought. She gave Mirele to Aunty and Uncle to live the life of a princess. Ma kept the dud – me – to live in poverty and misery. 'Hang the washing! Fetch the chicken! Not that one – the other one! *Nayn! Nayn!*

Nayn!' Each remembered command was punctuated in Rifke's mind with that terrible sound of the dress ripping.

Deanna's calloused hands grated at her skin as she brushed away her tears. Painfully she stood up, straightening her back slowly. She drew the back of her hand across her sweaty brow, and it was then that she saw through the scullery window that the gate to the courtyard had been left ajar. The evil old woman must have forgotten to chain and padlock it. Deanna rubbed her eyes to make sure it wasn't her imagination. She'd dreamed of escaping so many times. She stood absolutely still, listening, her heart pounding in her chest, and, when she was certain the old woman was not nearby, she untied her apron and flung it down on the wet floor. Hardly breathing, she gathered up her skirt and ran out of the scullery, across the courtyard and through the gate to freedom.

Rifke found herself moving towards the platforms.

'The train standing on Platform Six . . . calling at Krugersdorp, Potchefstroom, Klerksdorp, Christiania, Warrenton, Kimberley . . .' She only just caught the strains of the announcement above the clamour of people and trains. She began to run. Platform Four. Platform Five. 'Excuse me, please!' she dodged passengers, well-wishers, porters and baggage. Platform Six. A huge bubble of excitement swelled inside her.

'Is this definitely the Kimberley train?' a woman asked.

'*Ja, ja*, missus, it is. Leaving in one minute,' Rifke heard the stationmaster say.

Rifke reached the steps. For a split second she hesitated.

Kimberley.

She took a deep breath and scrambled up into the carriage.

'That's it, girlie, in you go,' the stationmaster said.

She could feel the heat of someone right behind her, pushing her in the small of her back and muttering, propelling her down the corridor. Outside on the platform, the stationmaster blew his whistle. Doors were slammed along the length of the train. The train lurched. Rifke felt a sharp thrill of something – excitement, panic, fear, joy. The train lurched again. They were off. She was going.

For a moment Rifke thought of Ma's face, creased with worry. She folded her arms. Too bad. Ma deserved to be punished. Anyway, it was only until the next morning. She'd telephone from Aunty and Uncle's house.

She didn't have a ticket. Well, so what? She could just dodge the inspector. What was the worst that could happen to her? Uncle and Aunty could just pay for her ticket or fine when she got to Kimberley.

The train snorted, and underneath her feet Rifke could feel its tendons. It was lengthening its stride, speeding up, freeing itself.

What could Ma do to her from that distance? Nothing. Nothing at all.

Rifke pressed herself against the wall of the carriage to let a group of people go past. The window next to her was slightly open. She let the wind catch her hair and cool her down.

Chapter Ten

The bustle in the corridor died down as passengers found their compartments and settled in. Rifke made her way down the length of the train, looking over her shoulder and listening out for the ticket inspector. She peered into open compartments. How cosy everyone looked. She caught a glimpse of the perfect family. The mother was reading to the two girls. The father was standing in the doorway to their compartment. He looked at Rifke without seeing her, and shut the door with a smart click. Rifke moved on.

'Is you lost, miss?' the railway attendant asked, looking over his stack of bedrolls at her.

'N-no. Thank you. I'm fine.' Rifke said, her skin prickling with panic. What if he asked to see her ticket? She had to think of something quickly. 'Um – is the toilet at the end of the corridor?'

'*Ja*, miss. You can't miss it. There, on the left.' He winked at her. 'Get in early before the after-dinner rush, hey?'

'Thanks,' Rifke said. She walked off, reminding herself to look confident.

Ma had always taught her to avoid public lavatories. There were gangs of germs in public toilets, all on the

payroll of the Angel of *Krankeyt*, all waiting to mob you the minute you entered. Ma even made Rifke crouch behind the big tree in Joubert Park rather than use the ladies'.

The door to the tiny train toilet was ajar. There was no one inside. Rifke hovered for a moment, her foot against the door.

'*Kaartjies, asseblief!*' Rifke heard the call of the inspector. She glanced over her shoulder. He was rattling the door of a compartment. 'Tickets, please!'

She recognized him from previous train journeys. He was the one with small eyes and a notebook he was always writing in. Rifke's heart pounded. She kicked open the toilet door and slammed it shut behind her. There were at least four compartments to go before he reached her end of the corridor.

'Tickets please . . . tickets . . .' She listened to him through the door, careful not to touch anything in the poky space, trying not to breathe in the smell of old urine. She'd be all right.

'Tickets, please!' He was outside the door. He rapped twice. 'Inspector here. Show me your ticket.'

Rifke was so startled she really did have to use the toilet. 'I-I'll be right out,' she said, trying hard not to come into contact with anything while at the same time needing to balance herself as the train swayed and swung on the tracks. Would he wait outside for her? If she stayed in a long time, would he give up and go away?

She held off from pushing her foot on the lever to flush the toilet.

He rapped at the door again. 'Your ticket. I is waiting.'

Rifke tried to slow her breathing. She had to come out, but he mustn't see how frightened she was. She flushed the toilet and washed her hands. Taking a deep breath, she opened the door.

'My parents have my ticket, *meneer*,' she said. 'Up the train. In the carriage before this one.' She wasn't used to lying. Her face was hot, and probably red too. 'They must have forgotten to show it to you.' She found herself nodding as if to confirm everything she said, hoping to convince him.

He stared at her, his little black eyes boring into hers. She held his gaze. 'OK . . .' He screwed-up his face. 'So what do they look like?' His notebook was already open in his hand, a pencil dangling out of it on a piece of string.

Rifke described each member of the perfect family, surprised at how easily the lie was flowing out of her.

The inspector put up his hand. He stared at her a moment longer and grunted. 'OK. You come with me to find them then.'

Oh my goodness, oh my goodness. Rifke's stomach churned and a stab of acid made her put her hands to her middle.

She had an idea.

'In a minute – I'll come in a minute,' she said to the

inspector. 'But I really – please – I have to go back into the lavatory first.'

'All right.' The inspector frowned. 'I remember those people. I will go talk to them. But you—'

Rifke didn't even wait to hear the end of his sentence. Still clutching her middle, she shuffled into the toilet and shut the door.

She heard his footsteps fading. Slowly she opened the door, her heart hammering. There was no sign of the inspector. She turned around. Behind her were doors leading to the next carriage. A notice had been stuck on the glass. '*Geen Ingang*. No admittance.' Beyond the doors, everything was dark. She hesitated for a split second. She couldn't go back back up the train. Then she yanked

the lever. It took all her strength to pull the door open. It made a loud sucking noise as it opened and then shut behind her. She slipped into the dead space between the two carriages, the floor swaying beneath her feet. She felt for the lever to let herself into the next carriage and heaved her shoulder against it to push it open. It slammed shut behind her.

It was evening now. The carriage was dark, and Rifke had to feel her way down the corridor. She was breathing quickly, and sweating. This part of the train was airless. It smelt of stale cigarettes. It was cold too. Rifke looked over her shoulder. The lights of the carriage she'd just left looked miles away. A different universe.

She kept moving down the long corridor, feverishly patting the left-hand wall, until her fingers felt an open doorway. She slid inside and tucked herself behind the door frame. She put her hand on her chest to calm her pounding heart and stood, stiff, listening for the suck of the door opening and the scuff of the inspector's feet along the corridor.

But there was only the sound of the train clacking out the rhythm of a never-ending poem. Rifke dared another glance down the passage. It was like looking through the wrong end of a telescope. There was nobody there, in that tiny, faraway lit space. The inspector must have given up. All at once, Rifke felt overwhelmingly tired. The train jolted. She stumbled in the direction of the seats and flopped down.

The leather upholstery was icy cold, and Rifke began to shiver. Drawing her feet on to the seat, she tucked herself into a corner. There was something pressing against her back, and when she felt behind her she was surprised to find the blue bag. She took it off, and put it down next to her. For once she was glad of the thick cardigan Ma had insisted on that morning. She pulled it around herself, stretching it over her legs as tightly as she could. It had been a long day. It was hard to believe she'd been with Aunty and Uncle Ber in Kimberley only yesterday. 'And back with them again tomorrow,' she murmured. She smiled and closed her eyes.

Chapter Eleven

Sometime in the night, the train screamed. The shriek of metal against metal and the grind and clang that followed jounced Rifke awake. Her eyes sprang wide open, but she couldn't see a thing.

'Ma!' she shouted.

She reached for Ma's body alongside hers, but her hands met only the cold flatness of the wall. She straightened up a little, her heart pounding and her mouth dry. It was a second or two before she remembered where she was. The night was still stuck to the train window. A long way from Kimberley then. Rifke took a few deep breaths and sat back on the seat, her arms wrapped round herself as she listened to the train's manoeuvring. 'They're coupling some carriages or something,' she said out loud, reassuring herself.

When, after some whining and squealing, the train took up its rhythm again, Rifke stretched out along the length of the seat. She plummeted back into sleep.

Deanna Durbin was in a dark, damp cave, crouching behind some rocks near the entrance. Every time she moved, her white peep-toe sandals slipped on the slimy floor. Around her head hundreds of bats were swirling, their high-pitched squeaks and the flap of their wings tormenting her, drawing closer and closer. She held her arms across her face, swatting them away, wanting to cry out but knowing that she shouldn't. Her heart was trembling like a trapped dove.

The cave was suffused with a warm, golden light. A pair of hands was reaching towards her. Deanna looked up. The bats had fled to the roof of the cave, where they fluttered like little bits of charred paper. She smiled, and her eyes glistened. 'Father! I knew you'd come. I knew you'd save me,' she said.

'It's Goldilocks! And she's sleeping in my bed.'

Rifke couldn't make sense of the voice that had broken into her lovely dream. She shook her head and kept her eyes squeezed tight, trying to call Deanna back.

'Sleeping Beauty, you mean. Let's see if a kiss will wake her up.'

It was another male voice. Now the bright light was a glare behind her eyelids, and hot breath on her face made Rifke open her eyes. The compartment lights were on. It took a moment to adjust to their brightness. The blurry image in front of her cleared. She was looking straight into someone's face. She jumped with shock and shrank as far back into the corner as possible.

'Who – who – what . . . ?' Her throat was dry and her voice came out tight. There were three men in the compartment, but their reflection in the train window made it seem as though there were more. Soldiers. Their khaki uniforms looked out of place against the photographs of gabled Cape Dutch homesteads on the walls. Rifke could

hear more male voices outside the compartment and the echo of boots in the corridor. What had happened? Why were there soldiers on the Kimberley train? She pulled the edges of her cardigan together, her heart thudding.

The soldier nearest to her leaned in closer, steadying himself with one hand against the wall of the compartment. The sun had blazed a red blistering weal over the bridge of his nose and his cheekbones.

'Move over, Baker. Let me get a good look at Goldilocks,' one of the other two soldiers said. Rifke felt his gaze travelling over her. It chilled her blood.

'Get lost, Janssen. I saw her first.'

The one called Baker shouldered Janssen out of the way and leaned in closer. He couldn't have been much older than Rifke. His swagger was at adds with the tentative look in his eyes. He was too close to her. She glanced at the entrance to the compartment. The door was open. She could make a dash for it. The third soldier must have noticed her look. He stepped over to the doorway and filled the frame. Rifke was finding it hard to breathe.

'What's your name?' Baker asked, his mouth close to Rifke's face. Drops of his spit landed on her cheek.

Silent and rigid, Rifke kept her eyes fixed downwards, forcing herself to focus on a smear of chocolate on the hem of her dress. Her heart was a tight fist in her chest.

'Hey, look, Baker. You've scared her. Her forehead's covered in sweat.' Janssen ducked round the other side of Baker and sat down next to her. The stiff cotton of his uniform grazed Rifke's leg. 'It's okay, baby,' he said. 'Let *me* take care of you.'

He was older than Baker, and there was a glint of a wedding band among the coarse black hair on his hand; for a moment Rifke thought she might be able to trust him. But then she saw that huge hand coming down like a giant hairy spider towards her knee.

'Don't touch me!' she shouted. She leaped to her feet. Knocked her bag off the seat. The cigarette box flew out and skidded across the floor. With a graceful twirl it stopped at the boots of the soldier in the doorway. The cigarettes spilled out in a fan.

'No!' Rifke scrabbled to the floor, but the soldier swung his boot out, cornered the cigarettes and scooped them up.

'Give them back!' She swiped at them, but he laughed and held them out of her reach. 'They're mine!' she shouted.

'Not any more.' He pulled a lighter out of his top pocket and lit one.

The familiar smell filled the compartment, and for a moment, Rifke was transfixed.

'Here, catch, you two!' he called to the others, and threw a cigarette to each of them.

'Give us a light, *boetie*,' Baker said.

The soldier moved to offer the lit end of his cigarette, leaving the doorway empty. Rifke saw her chance. Grab-

bing her canvas bag, she whipped past him and out into the corridor.

'Should we go after her?' Janssen asked.

'No, man. She can't go far. Let Sarge catch her,' Baker said, and they all laughed.

The corridor was empty, but she could hear clattering and the rumble of men's voices coming from the compartments. She paused for a second, paralysed. She had to hide. But where?

Chapter Twelve

A raucous laugh came from somewhere behind her. Rifke bolted. The soldiers in the compartments she passed were blurs. On she ran. Down the corridors. Through three carriages. Pulling and dragging open the linking doors. Letting them shut behind her.

Through the final set of glass doors into a stubby little section. No passenger compartments; a dead-end look about it – the back of the train. Three doors: the exit door and two others, one of them ajar. Rifke stopped. Glanced around. It seemed deserted. Trying to still her breath, she looked through the open door. Guard's cabin. Syrupy dance music winding out of a wireless, curls of steam rising from a full cup of tea. Someone would be coming back. Soon.

Rifke darted towards the other door. She tried the handle. It was stiff. She was tired, her arms and hands weak.

'Come on. Open!'

The door wasn't locked: no keyhole. It had to open. There were voices. She looked over her shoulder. Through the glass doors, someone – a man, his back to her – talking to someone else. He turned slightly, as if to move into Rifke's section. Rifke ducked down and went at the door with increased urgency. She rattled and turned the handle at the same time, using both hands. She had to get in. There was nowhere else to go.

'Come on, come on!'

A hefty kick, and the door gave way suddenly and swung open. Rifke hurtled into darkness. She fell against something huge and solid, a crate of some sort. Her knees scraped its rough surface as her legs buckled and she hit the floor. She slid across and pushed the door firmly shut.

Rubbing her smarting knees, she leaned against the crate. Her breath came in judders, and tears stung her eyes.

'Stop,' she told herself. 'Stop. Mustn't cry. They'll hear.'

She dashed her eyes against her arms, wiping them on the coarse knit of her cardigan. It smelt strongly of her father's cigarettes, and that brought more tears. The soldiers had stolen the last bit of him she had. Of course she could buy another box of Cape to Cairo cigarettes, but a fresh box wouldn't come with the knowledge that his fingers had trawled over the contents as he'd removed a cigarette and then replaced the box in the inside pocket of his jacket.

Rifke wiped her nose on her sleeve. If only she hadn't taken his box with her that morning. But then it occurred to her – who knew what the soldiers might have done to her if they hadn't been distracted by the cigarettes? The cigarettes had saved her. *Her father* had saved her. The thought was as comforting as having him there with her in that dark storeroom.

'Soon be in Kimberley,' she whispered, and it was as though he'd reassured her himself.

She touched her knees again. One of them was bleeding. Rifke pressed her dress against it to soak up the blood. She knew Aunty would immediately get out her enormous tin box of bandages and medicines. What must Rifke's Lithuanian grandmother have been like to have produced Ma and Aunty with all their armoury against illness and ailments? Soon Aunty would cover her knees in Mercurochrome. The splashes of scarlet would look far worse than the wounds. Farieda would bring her sweet black tea in one of those Russian glasses, Alfred would make sucking noises of sympathy with his false teeth, and Uncle Ber would pull out a chair and a footstool for her. Thinking about them made Rifke feel calmer.

Ma. The thought of her was a splinter of guilt, snagging Rifke's conscience for a second. She tossed her head. Nothing had changed. One night of worry for Ma. That was all it was. And no more than Ma deserved. Of course, when Rifke telephoned from the house there'd be endless ranting and raving, and Ma would quote from the Ten Commandments and, as usual, she'd find some way to blame Aunty. But maybe Ma would learn something too. Maybe she'd learn not to be so difficult and rigid.

Rifke eased herself into a more comfortable position and looked around. The small compartment smelt of burnt dust and oil, overlaid with the tang of oranges and the sweet mustiness of apples. Rectangular grilles near the ceiling let in a stingy scrap of moonlight that allowed Rifke to make out a series of shelves and racks arranged in regular parallels. It was a storeroom. As her eyes became used to the darkness, Rifke distinguished packages and boxes stacked on the shelves, names of farms stamped on their sides – Slange Rivier, Driekoppen, Kruit Vlei. Empty now, it seemed, by the way they were sliding about and clattering against each other. Only the large crate in the centre, the one she'd fallen against, was unmoving and solid.

Footsteps out in the corridor. The guard was back. He was next door, shadowing some crooner on the wireless. Trying not to hit her knees on anything, Rifke shuffled behind the crate. If he did open the storeroom, he wouldn't be able to see her crouching there.

What time was it? She wasn't wearing a watch and couldn't tell from the light sifting in from the overhead grilles. Two o'clock? Maybe three? She was leaden with tiredness. Ravenous too. Her stomach growled. She remembered she hadn't eaten all the chocolate she'd bought at the station. She reached for the canvas bag and opened it.

The sour, metallic stench of dead chicken rose from the bag like a hand and smacked Rifke in the face. She gasped, then clamped her hand in front of her mouth, hoping the guard hadn't heard. His crooning ambled on without stopping. It was OK. He hadn't. Quickly she rummaged in the bag, found the remains of her chocolate and rolled the opening of the bag to seal in the stink. If he did come in, Rifke mused, all she would have to do to overpower him would be to open the bag and wave it at him. She bit off a chunk of chocolate. Too bad she hadn't thought of that with those soldiers. She smiled at the thought of the three of them passing out after just one whiff, and that made her feel better. Some of the girls at school had romantic dreams about being swept off their feet by a man in uniform. Wait until she told Betty and Veronica about those she'd just met. The memory of the hairy hand made her shudder. One thing was certain, *she* was never ever going to knit another sock for the war effort.

She leaned back against the crate and strained to hear what the guard was up to next door. The radio station had moved to a church programme, and the man was humming along to the hymn being broadcast. The dreary, never-ending service blended with the train's rhythm, and although she fought to keep her eyes open, it wasn't long before she drifted into a skimming sort of sleep – a half-sleep in which everything that had happened that day swirled around and merged and became half real, half dreamed.

'C'mon, Elias! It's an even bigger crate this time. Give us a hand with it.'

Rifke stiffened. Someone was coming in. The door swung open. Judging by the wedge of light cutting into the gloom of the storeroom, it was morning. Rifke blinked a couple of times. Morning. They must be near Kimberley now. Something was different. The train wasn't moving. The train must be *in* Kimberley. She grabbed her bag and stood up. She had to get out.

'Whoa!' The guard leaped backwards, his hand against his chest. 'Jesus, man, what the hell are you doing in here, girlie?' He leaned forward, screwing up his eyes as if to make sure he was really seeing her. 'Elias! Come here, man!'

'I – er – I must . . .' Rifke felt the crust of dried blood on her knees cracking as she moved quickly round the crate. 'I – please – I need to get off here.' The train was panting, raring to go.

A tall black man appeared in the doorway. He too did a double take.

'Hoo, *baas*. A woman person! What's she doing here?'

'That's a good question, man.' The guard raised his eyebrows. 'What the hell *are* you doing here? It's strictly against the rules.'

The two men were blocking the door. The train lurched.

'Please – don't let the train go yet. I've got to get off.'

The guard had removed his cap and was scratching

85

the back of his head. Elias was staring at her. She jostled her way between them and ran out of the storeroom.

'Hey, girlie – where are you going? I don't think –'

Rifke made a dash for the exit door. She flung it open and launched herself at the platform.

Chapter Thirteen

It wasn't Kimberley.

No milling people in smart clothes, no stacked luggage, no porters, no muffled announcements. Only a narrow platform with a tumbledown shack. It was early morning, but the sun was already switched to full power. There was nothing around except orange earth, low scrub and spiteful thorn trees. Acres – miles – of it. Far away a faint outline suggested a mountain range.

Rifke could not believe what she was seeing. She'd definitely got on to the train to Kimberley, yet Kimberley had disappeared. Sometime during the night it had evaporated. She turned around, sand grinding under the soles of her shoes. And the train – where were all the carriages? Now there was only the engine and the stumpy little storeroom section.

'Mister!' she shouted, the heat of panic radiating from her, her dress suddenly sticking to her chest. '*Meneer*!'

She scrambled back up the steps and into the train. The men were dragging the huge crate out of the storeroom. She grabbed the guard by his sleeve.

'Where are we – I thought – Mister, I need –' She could hardly get the words out. 'Please. Help me. I want – Kimberley.'

He turned. 'Kimberley?' he said, his eyes opening wide. 'Oh, no, girlie. This isn't Kimberley. The—'

'Yes, yes, I know.' Rifke interrupted him. Why did he have to speak so slowly? 'But I just need to know where –'

The guard put his hand up.

'If you will just wait a little bit, I will explain, miss. The Kimberley part of the train left us hours ago.' He checked his watch. '*Ja*, at twenty-three thirty-three, to be precise. Just before Klerksdorp it was, hey, Elias? It was at that time that the military boarded. And then *they* left us at—'

Rifke nodded. 'Yes, yes, I understand, *meneer*.' She couldn't keep the words from spilling out. 'But how am I going to get to Kimberley now? I mean, are we far away? Can this train go there? Where are we now?'

'Slow down, miss.' He set down the rope he was holding and sighed. 'We are many, many miles away from Kimberley.' He spoke as though he were talking to a five-year-old. 'Hundreds of miles away. This train is now going straight to the depot, my girl.'

'But what – what am I going to do?' Rifke's stomach twisted.

The guard scratched his head again. The engine's whistle sounded and smoke belched out and drifted past the window.

'We must better hurry, *baas*,' Elias said, and bent to push the crate again.

The guard turned away from Rifke and picked up the rope.

'Well . . .' He chewed on his grey moustache for a moment. 'I s'pose you *could* travel with the train to the depot . . . and from there maybe there will be a way to get to Kimberley. But –' he took a sharp intake of breath – 'there will be hell to pay when they sees you at the depot. Many, many questions to answer. Questions for me and for you, girlie.' He flung the rope over his shoulder and heaved the crate towards him.

Rifke didn't like the sound of that. But what choice did she have?

'Or,' he continued, panting a bit, 'you could go to Mevrou Whatsername – van Niel – and ask her to help you. Her farm is somewhere around here. This is her crate so she'll be coming to collect it. Mind out of the way now, miss.'

'How far away is the depot from here?' Rifke stepped back on to the platform and stood to one side as the two men manoeuvred the crate towards the exit door.

'Many, many miles.' The guard grunted. 'Three hours.'

'And is it on the way to Kimberley?'

'*Ag* no man, girlie.' The guard gave a dry laugh. 'They is in opposite directions.' He turned his attention back to the crate. 'OK, Elias. Careful now.' They hefted it on to the platform. 'Every two months we do this, and I swear the bladdy thing gets heavier and heavier, hey, Elias?'

'*Ja, baas!*' Elias wiped his forehead with his forearm. 'Shoo, it's hot already. And, *baas*, there is something smelling round here. Maybe something went bad in the storeroom. I must better go see what it is.' He climbed back into the train.

The guard wrinkled his nose, swivelling his head in all directions. '*Ja*, you is right, Elias. Something is stinking very bad round here. Things go off very, very quick in the heat.'

Rifke hid the bag behind her back.

'Now what was I doing?' continued the guard. He thought for a second, then took a notebook and pencil out of his pocket, ticked something off and replaced them. He climbed the steps into the train.

'Quick now, girlie. We's off now. Quick, quick. Make up your mind.' The train lurched again and hissed. 'You staying or going?' He leaned out of the train, the door still open, his hand on the inner handle.

Rifke rubbed her forehead with the heel of her hand. She was breathing quickly. Stay or go. Stay or go. Hell to pay at the depot. Miles and miles away. Stay. Go. No, stay. Mrs van Niel. A woman. Better. A farm. She'd have a truck. She could drive her to Kimberley. The train gave a long high whistle. Rifke wiped her hand over her face. Her skin was slick.

'Stay. I'll stay.'

The guard nodded, slammed the door and, stretching far out of the open window, he waved at the driver. There

was a split second before the train's pistons began to turn.

No. No! What had she been thinking? There was no one here.

'No!' She screamed. 'No! Take me with you!'

But the engine swallowed her words as huge swells of smut-spotted steam billowed into her face. She ran after the train, waving and shouting, the blue canvas bag flying from her fist. 'Stop! Stop! I've changed my mind!'

No one heard her, and soon the train was just a cloud moving along the zip-like track, getting smaller and smaller as the sound of its panting faded to nothing.

Rifke stood where she was for a minute or two. She was alone. Alone on a dusty ridge of earth that passed for a platform, in the middle of the *bundu*, with only a crate for company. Alone – for the first time in her life. No one even knew where she was – apart from the guard and Elias. And they'd probably forgotten about her already.

Panic rippled through her again.

What if Mrs Whatever never came for her crate?

What if she didn't even exist?

What if she did exist but only came in a week's time?

What if she refused to help Rifke and left her there to die of starvation and thirst and vultures came and pecked at her bony legs before she'd even finished dying?

Chapter Fourteen

Fingers trembling, Rifke pulled off her cardigan and wiped the back of her neck with it.

Deep breaths, she told herself. She snorted back a trickle of snot and tried to square her shoulders. 'It'll be all right,' she said out loud, just to hear a voice. But it came out wobbly, and that made her feel even more desolate.

She buried her face in the cardigan, breathing in the faint traces of Ma's washing soap and the cigarettes, as well as the stronger smells of dust and sweat. And dead chicken.

That damn chicken. She needed to get rid of it. She looked around. There was no rubbish bin, and nothing that could be used as one. Perhaps she could just dump it somewhere: no one would know. She walked to the end of the platform and half stepped, half slid down. The sand here was looser. She used her sandal to kick out a hollow.

As she opened the bag, she took a deep breath and held it. Could someone die of a bad smell? The chicken lay there, plump and dead and still in its brown paper wrapper. Dov Kossoff had dropped it into her bag only the day before. A year ago, it seemed. The polonies were there too, but fine – not off. She'd keep them. Farieda made the best polony omelettes, and they were Mirele's favourite breakfast. So, holding back the cylinders of smoked meat, Rifke dropped the chicken into its shallow grave, scuffed a bit of sand over it and started to climb back up on to the platform. She stopped with one foot on the embankment.

She couldn't do it. She couldn't leave that stupid kosher chicken to its fate out here in the middle of the *bundu*. Yes, it was already dead, but it was supposed to have ended up in the dented roasting tin that had come with Ma from Lithuania, squashed up next to a heap of potatoes and carrots. Ma should have been sucking the juices out of its neck that evening. Rifke shuddered.

The chicken, like Rifke, was out of its usual environment and abandoned to who knew what end. She sighed. Holding her breath again, she dug the chicken out of its ditch and put it back into her bag. It would be a kind of talisman. As long as she kept hold of the chicken, she would be safe.

'And besides,' Rifke said out loud, 'I chose that chicken. It was killed because I said so. It shouldn't go to waste.' She smiled. 'Atticus can have it.'

She hooked the bag over her arm and slid and clambered her way back on to the platform, then wandered over to the crate. Where in all this emptiness did that woman live?

The writing on the side of the rough wood was large and bold. All it said was: 'Mevrou van Niel. Driemieliesfontein.'

93

Was that the name of the farm or the name of this town? It sounded more like a town name. The sender must have been really confident that Mevrou van Niel would get the crate to put only that on it. Everyone must know her. The thought was comforting. Yes, Mevrou van Niel would sweep up in her car – no, the farm truck – a jaunty scarf round her neck and sunglasses perched on the end of her nose. She'd bring a couple of strong farmhands to lift the crate into the back of the truck. After a moment's surprise at finding a girl on the station, she'd wink at Rifke and open the passenger door of the truck.

'Hop in, girlie!' she'd say. 'We'll nip back to the farm, drop off the box, cool ourselves down with a lovely cold soda and then I'll zip you over to Kimberley. You'll be back with your uncle and aunt in no time at all.'

Rifke smiled. Her vision of Mevrou van Niel's haven in the middle of the country merged a little with the fantasy of her father's white verandaed mansion, and Aunty and Uncle's house too. She could almost smell the honeysuckle winding over the trelliswork and feel the delicious cool of the house as she followed Mevrou van Niel through the front door and into the kitchen, where a jug of something pink sparkled on a tray.

Rifke was too hot to feel hungry, but the thought of a cold drink reminded her just how dry and gummy her mouth felt. If only she'd asked the guard for a drink of water.

She looked around. Perhaps there was a tap or a pump

somewhere. She made her way to the tumbledown shack. The panes of its only window had long since disappeared and its door swung on one hinge. If she'd been hoping for some shade, there was none to be found there: all that remained of the roof was a splintered board or two. No sign of any plumbing, let alone a pump. A dry sigh of hot wind lifted the shreds of what must once have been a train timetable.

Rifke wandered to the opposite edge of the platform. A rough dirt track, wide enough for a vehicle, emerged from the dusty scrub and joined the platform. Mevrou van Niel's truck would come from there, she thought.

She needed shade. Rifke passed her tongue over her lips. They were dry, beginning to crack. Shielding her throbbing head with the canvas bag, she walked back to the crate. It felt to Rifke like an old friend. She crouched against it, facing the direction of the rough road, and draped her cardigan along one of its edges and over her head like an awning. After a minute she threw the canvas bag out. The heat was bad enough; the smell made it worse.

'Please come, Mevrou van Niel. Please come soon,' she whispered.

Chapter Fifteen

Her ears tuned to hear the growl of a truck engine, Rifke didn't at first recognize the twittering sounds. She ducked out from under the cardigan and stood up. The fierce light burned her eyes. Those high-pitched sounds were naggingly familiar – like children in a playground. But there was no one there – the landscape seemed exactly the same as it had before. Apart from the thorn trees and the dull scrub, there was nothingness. Baked, searing nothingness.

Rifke wiped the sweat trickling down the backs of her knees with her hands, and rubbed her hands on her damp dress. She looked up at the hard blue sky, trying to come up with a prayer. Failing – her head too hot, too heavy – she turned to burrow back under her shelter.

Something caught her eye. A tiny, dark wiggle in the distance, far down a track between the thorn trees. It grew bigger in the liquid light, split into separate blobs and then into three . . . people. Rifke blinked a couple of times just to make sure. Yes, definitely people. She ran to the edge of the platform.

'Hello!' Her voice rasped in her paper-dry throat. She waved, then clambered down the ridge towards them. Thank goodness. They must be coming for the crate.

'Hello!' she tried to call again, waiting for them to draw nearer.

They were children.

Two white boys, of about ten and eleven, with long, scruffy hair and loose, faded clothes, and a very small boy of about two. He was neither black nor white, but a caramel colour Rifke had never seen before, with curious auburn, tightly curled hair and nothing covering his lower half. The older boys were pulling a low trolley with a wooden thing inside it, shrieking as the little one toddled around them poking at the backs of their legs with a long stalk of grass. They hadn't spotted Rifke yet.

'Excuse me – um, I'm – hello,' she said, taking a small step forward.

The baby saw her first. He screamed and grabbed the leg of one of the others, who looked up and nudged the arm of the third boy. For what seemed like ages they stared at Rifke, unblinking and wary.

She made an awkward gesture with her hand. 'I'm Rifke,' she said. 'I – I came with the crate – I mean, I came with the train and I got out with the crate . . .'

Still the boys stared. The baby whimpered and reached to be picked up.

'You know,' Rifke swallowed and ploughed on, 'the crate, the big box for Mevrou van Niel of Driemielies-fontein? Do you—'

'Mevrou van Niel?' The tallest boy spoke with recognition in his voice. Relieved, Rifke prattled on. 'Yes.

Apparently, she's expecting this delivery. Gets one every two months. So, I'd be really grateful if you'd take me to her and—'

'*Wat doen jy hier?*' the boy asked. He was frowning. The other white boy looked at her through screwed-up eyes.

Rifke understood Afrikaans better than she could speak it, but she would have a go. Taking a deep breath, she explained in stiff textbook sentences what she was doing there. A smile passed between the older boys, and Rifke flushed with embarrassment and anger. At least she was *trying* to speak their language.

The younger boy whispered something to the other, who nodded. They moved towards Rifke, the baby pottering along beside them. Then, without catching her eye, they walked straight past.

Rifke stood for a minute, staring at their backs as they made their way towards the platform. How rude, she thought, wiping her forehead on her arm. Well, they weren't going to ignore her so easily. They must come from somewhere, and she would follow them whether or not they wanted her to.

After a minute or two of watching the older two boys battling with the crate, she went over to help. Together they heaved and shoved it to the edge of the platform, down the embankment and on to the wooden thing that turned out to be a ramp. The crate kept threatening to teeter out of control and crash on to one of them. Once the crate was installed in the trolley, one of the bigger boys muttered a grudging thank-you in Afrikaans, while the other used his outretched leg to keep the baby out of the way.

The journey out of there was hard going. The older boys forged ahead of Rifke. They struggled to move the crate along the sandy track; the wheels of the trolley kept seizing up. Every few minutes they had to stop to clear a way for it.

Rifke's arms were aching and her legs felt as though they would give way at any moment. The sun beat her head; its fierce heat plastered her hair to her scalp and her dress to her skin. Inside her socks, her toes slid against each other, while her shoes kept filling with the gritty ochre earth. And from the canvas bag slung across her back, the dead chicken gave off its rank stink. The boys had noticed it. They flapped their hands in front of their noses when Rifke drew close to them, and whispered in each other's ears. But she was past caring.

They passed a low-lying building partly hidden by trees. A tiny house, a cottage really, smoke-blackened along one gable and over part of its tin roof. The fire hadn't reached its door, which was still intact, as were most of the windows' little panes. It looked sorry for itself. The boys didn't even glance in its direction. Thank goodness, Rifke thought. She was glad Mevrou van Niel didn't live there.

'How . . . much . . . further?' she asked in Afrikaans, in a wheezy rasp that scraped her throat.

The boys didn't answer. One of them gave a vague wave, not looking back at her. Rifke was desperate to sit, to sink down in the hot soil. But the boys wouldn't wait for her, she knew that, and no way was she going to be left behind for a second time. She knew, too, that if she allowed herself to stop, she would never get up again.

The baby, who'd been plodding ahead of the trolley, was slowing down. His bandy legs faltered and he plopped on to his bottom in the sand. He wailed in a mixture of Afrikaans and some other language. The bigger boys just kept on dragging and pushing the crate. When they drew close to him, one of them said something and the baby clung on to his shorts for a few paces. When he couldn't keep up, he stood teetering on the path, his face curled with distress. Rifke moved over to him.

'Come,' she said in English, too exhausted to try Afrikaans. 'Come . . . I will . . . help you.' She held out her hand.

He turned away from her. 'Piet!' he called out. 'Hendrik!' His voice was hoarse as he began to cry, and snot bubbled out of his nostrils.

The boys were disappearing down the track. Rifke panicked. She scooped the baby out of the sand, finding strength from nowhere. He screamed and kicked and flailed his arms about.

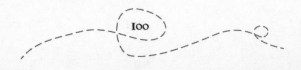

'No, baby,' she said firmly. 'You just . . . have to . . . come with me.'

She felt a bit awkward about the no pants and the patches of sand stuck to his bottom, so she clutched him round his waist and wedged him above her hip. He struggled a bit more. They were both so slippery with sweat, she almost dropped him.

'Stop it!' she shouted, surprising herself and the child. He looked up at her. She'd never seen eyes quite that colour – tawny, between green and brown. 'Stop wriggling,' she said more quietly. She looked away, embarrassed by his stare.

Bit by bit the baby made himself more at home on her hip. By the time the sandy track joined a rutted drive, the baby was sucking his thumb while gripping a strand of Rifke's hair. She swatted away the flies that circled them – drawn both by the decomposing chicken in her bag and the baby's snotty face.

The ground sloped gently downwards. Piet and Hendrik sped up.

'Are we . . . there yet?' Rifke called out.

The boys seemed not to hear her. The path swept round quite suddenly and Rifke found herself at the entrance to a tree-lined avenue, her gaze sweeping down the long drive. Rifke stopped. There, way down, at its end, was a large single-storey house with graceful gables and symmetrically placed windows. Its white facade shone out in the afternoon sunshine against the dark greens and browns of the trees leading to it. It could have come out of a picture book or one of the framed photographs in the train compartments, advertising holidays in the Cape. She laughed out loud. Civilization at last.

'Thank goodness!' she said. 'Not long before I'm on my way to Kimberley again. Come on, baby.' Hoisting him higher on her hip, she began to walk faster.

Part Two

Chapter Sixteen

As they drew nearer to the house, Rifke saw that it wasn't in great condition. Its thatched roof was bald in places. The facade, which had seemed such a dazzling white from afar, was shabby and grey where patches of plaster were missing. Rusty tears ran down from the corners of the windows. What a shame, Rifke thought. It must have been grand and gracious once. Now it was like a neglected old lady.

She looked around. Where were Piet and Hendrik? They'd left the crate in front of the house and disappeared. Apart from the whirring of locusts and the odd bird call, it was silent. Still holding the baby, Rifke moved towards the front door. It was set slightly back between two fluted pillars and below a large, many-paned window. She lifted the knocker and banged on the door. A dull sound. Somewhere a dog barked. She waited a minute or two, then took a few steps back. The window above the door was too high to see into. She peered into the windows on either side. The rooms were dark.

'Hello!' she called. 'Is anyone there?'

Wriggling on her hip, the baby glanced at her, then looked over her shoulder. The place was too still. The hairs rose on the back of Rifke's neck. Was someone watching her? She swung round. There were a few outbuildings to the left of the house, about twenty or thirty feet away. Perhaps they had once been the servants' quarters. They looked abandoned now. She looked around again. Not even the leaves on the trees were stirring.

Without warning, the baby pushed against her chest. 'Ow!' she shouted.

He slithered down to the ground. Landing on all fours, he righted himself and toddled in the direction of the outbuildings. A door opened just as he reached the first one. A muffled voice, a woman's, shouted from inside in a language Rifke didn't understand, and the baby began to howl. He was pulled inside and the door was slammed.

So there *was* someone around. Rifke wiped her forehead with her sleeve and made her way over to where the baby had gone. Two of the outbuildings were no more than shells: doors and windows gone, just used to store farm implements.

'Hello!' Rifke called out as she knocked on the door of the third. The baby was still howling inside, but there was no sound from the woman.

'Please.' She rattled the handle. 'I know you're in there.' Her voice was hoarse. What kind of a place was this? What was wrong with the people round here? She swatted away the flies that were circling the canvas bag. 'Please open the door.'

She was feeling light-headed. Sighing, she leaned her forehead for a moment against the blistered paint and smacked the door with her palm. It left a sweaty smear.

There must be other people living there. Perhaps they were round the back of the house.

Rifke turned and made her way down a shady path between the outbuildings and the main house, stumbling over broken toys and an old feeding trough.

Her head was spinning. She hardly took in the fields and farm buildings and the now more defined mountain range ahead of her. To her right was a high metal gate leading to the back garden of the main house. A few rusty chairs and a rickety table were grouped under a tree. The gate whined as she let herself through.

'Is anyone here?' Her legs were weak. She tripped over some large animal bones, moon-white and jagged. Had to grab hold of an old metal chair to steady herself. There was washing on the line. Wet. French windows in the centre of the house were open.

'Come out . . . someone. Please. I just . . . want to go to Kimberley.'

Her throat was dry, tight. Must sit. Water. She sank on to the chair. Head throbbing. So sore.

A scuttle of claws on a wooden floor. Something crouching low. Dark against the darkness of the doorway. Atticus. No, but just like Atticus.

'Here, boy!' she tried to call. She put out her hand as

Mirele had done, her lips too dry to make the kissy-tutty noises Aunty did to call Atticus over.

The dog made a throaty noise. It paused, its head craning forward, one paw raised. When it lowered itself to the ground, Rifke turned away. Dazed and dehydrated, she rested her head in her hands and closed her eyes.

A snarl ripped the air.

Rifke jumped, her eyes snapping open. An enormous, savage, growling heap of animal flew at her, nose pulled back and mouth peeled open, huge yellow teeth in a vicious grin and strings of saliva flying out the sides. Rifke scrambled to stand on the chair.

'No!' Her hoarse cry did nothing to stop the dog. Its claws scraped her legs as it hurled itself at her again and again, barking, snarling and growling more and more loudly. Rifke kicked out at it. Its jaws snapped at her foot. 'No! Stop it!' The chair rocked and tilted backwards. 'Help!' Distract it. Quick. The canvas bag banged against her side. Of course. She pulled it round, dug the chicken out and lobbed it across the garden.

The smell reached the dog's nose. It stopped, its paws still on the edge of the chair. Raised its head. Sniffed.

'Good dog,' Rifke said in a wheedling voice. 'Fetch.'

A mistake. The sound of her voice reminded the dog she was there. With a roar he leaped at her again. She pulled away. The chair tipped backwards. Rifke's legs flew up and her head smashed against the sun-baked ground. With every bark, the dog pumped hot breath on to her face. She rolled herself into a ball, burying her head in her arms. Her ears blocked, she waited for the dog's first bite.

Nothing happened. She unblocked her ears. The dog was still barking, but in a strangled way. Rifke looked up. It took her a few seconds to focus. Someone was dragging the now gasping and wheezing dog away from her. Rifke rubbed the back of her head. She blinked. A clatter of metal and a click. She could see now that he was a boy of about nineteen or twenty, with the same scruffy look as Piet and Hendrik. He was tall and broad, with tousled fair hair that fell forward as he bent to clip the dog's collar to a length of chain attached to a pole.

'*Hou jou bek!*' the boy shouted.

The dog was secure. Rifke sat up. Her head was pounding now.

'*Goeiedag,*' he called out to Rifke. 'Or shall I say, "good day"?'

Tossing his hair out of his eyes, the boy walked over to her. He wore faded shorts and a loose shirt, mended along the sleeve, with a white-and-red beaded necklace at his neck. He was barefoot. His skin was tanned. He put his right hand out towards Rifke. The hairs on his muscly forearm were gold.

'Rifke Lubetkin,' she tried to say, but it came out as a croak. She offered her right hand. A flush rose up her neck and took over her face. He grabbed her hand. She'd thought he'd introduce himself, but he didn't. Instead, he hoisted her to her feet. But her legs wouldn't hold her up, and they folded beneath her.

'Whoa!' he said, and caught her. He swung Rifke into a horizontal position, so that one of his arms was around her shoulders, and the other under her legs.

'I will take you now inside.'

Even in her feeble state, Rifke was aware of that hand, hot and dry against her skin, with a touch of roughness.

'Um . . . thank you . . . I think I'm OK now,' she croaked again. She struggled to get free, but he tightened his grip. He was moving towards the house. He stopped.

'Hell, man. What is that stink?' He bent over her and sniffed. 'It's not you, is it?'

Another blush rushed up Rifke's neck and swarmed her face. If only she could creep into a shell like a tortoise. If only she weren't here at all.

Her head was hurting so much. She just wanted Aunty and her big tin of medicines. She squeezed her eyes shut. Don't cry.

'And what's that bladdy dog got now?'

Rifke heard the snap of bones as the dog ripped into the chicken.

'Jesus, a dead chicken. A stinking dead chicken! *En waarvandaan het daardie ding gekom?*' He shook Rifke in his arms. 'Where the hell did that come from? And I could say also – where the hell did you come from, hey?'

'Train . . . wrong . . . Kimberley . . .' Rifke's voice tailed off.

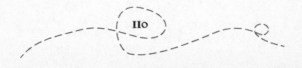

'*Ag*, never mind, you can tell us later,' the boy said.

The sudden cold inside the house was a shock. Rifke's skin sprang goose pimples as they moved through the dark rooms.

'Moeder!' the boy called. 'Mother! Where are you?'

Chapter Seventeen

'*Wat is dit, Anton? Is iets verkeerd? Het iets met Piet of Hendrik gebeur?*'

Her footsteps came from behind them. It was a woman's voice, high and breathy.

'No, Mother. Nothing is wrong. Piet and Hendrik is fine. It is a girl. I found her outside. She needs water.' He laughed. 'To drink *and* to bath.'

The mother drew closer, incredulous.

'A girl?' she said in Afrikaans.

Rifke's eyes were taking their time to adjust to the dark. She blinked a few times. The mother took a few steps back, her face a pale oval.

'How did she get here? I did not hear a car.'

'I don't know. I just found her there in the garden.'

'Put. . . me down. Please.' she croaked. 'I'm . . . OK.' Rifke thrashed her legs about. Anton shook his head and pressed his hand into her thigh more firmly.

'Take her to the kitchen,' the mother said.

Her footsteps followed them down a passage and through a doorway. Anton moved towards a long wooden table and set Rifke down on the bench in front of it, her legs sprawling. It was easier to see now. Light drifted in through the small windowpanes that made up the huge sash window. What was this place? Some sort of a museum? Rifke felt as though she'd been carried back into another century. An open fireplace with some kind of iron oven next to it dominated the room, together with a deep stone sink and a pump. A pair of ancient cupboards leaned towards each other on the uneven floor.

Rifke rested her elbows on the table and held her head. There was a gurgle and splash as water was pumped. Anton nudged her shoulder. He was holding out a handle-less cup.

'Drink,' he ordered. He sat down next to Rifke. So close she could feel the heat from his body.

'Thank you. *Dankie*,' she said. The cold water burned her mouth and throat. Her teeth rang with pain.

'Ask her, Anton – what is she doing here?' the mother said. She was standing near the window, her forearms across her chest.

'You can ask her yourself, Mother. Your English is good enough.'

Rifke looked at the woman over the top of the cup. She was tall, wide-shouldered, like her son. But she was gaunt. The light coming from around her sharpened the contours of her face. The ridges of her cheekbones were a preview of her skull. She was wearing an almost floor-length gathered skirt made of some drab material and a man's long-sleeved shirt buttoned up to the neck. She held a sock stretched over a darning egg in one hand, and, even while she was looking at Rifke, she fingered the hole in the sock's heel with the other. A big darning needle had been threaded through the shirt pocket in readiness.

'*Nee*,' she said, her brows dipping into a V, and shifted her feet on the floor. Her heavy man's ankle boots clattered against the rough surface.

Rifke took a few more sips of the water and placed the cup quietly down on the table. She didn't want to make the woman more hostile. Rifke wondered if the crate were still where the boys had left it. Presumably Mevrou van Niel would come here to collect her crate and, when she did, Rifke wanted to be sure to get a lift with her out of this godforsaken place.

'Um . . .' she began, her voice clearer now. She was conscious of both pairs of eyes on her. 'Is Driemieliesfontein far from here? Do you know when Mevrou van Niel will come to collect her crate?' She spoke careful Afrikaans, picking her way through the simple sentences as if on stepping stones. She'd stopped feeling faint; the water had helped. But her head still hurt.

Anton and his mother glanced at each other. Didn't they understand her Afrikaans? She repeated it. There was a moment's silence.

'Tell her, Anton,' the woman then said.

Anton leaned into Rifke, his leg brushing against hers. 'This is Driemieliesfontein. My mother is Mevrou van Niel.'

Rifke gasped, staring at this wary woman with her

scraped-back hair and ugly clothes. Where was the fashionable farmer's wife, her gleaming truck and the sparkling drink? Was this rundown, austere house really Driemieliesfontein?

'What you want with my mother?' Anton asked. His green eyes stared right into Rifke's, without blinking. 'What you doing here?'

Rifke took a deep breath. She explained in English what had happened, leaving out the details about the argument with Ma, not having a ticket and running away from the soldiers. To them, it was simply a case of the wrong train. Not to be rude, Rifke tore her gaze away from Anton's now and then to include his mother in the explanation. Mevrou van Niel said nothing. She gave a slight nod when Rifke reached the point in the story where she'd arrived at the house with the crate.

'So what now, hey, girlie?' Anton asked. He rubbed his jaw, his fingers rasping against the gold stubble.

'Well, I was hoping . . . um . . . someone could drive me . . . to . . .' Rifke's expectation that she would be whisked off to Kimberley seemed suddenly naive and unreasonable, and she could hardly bear to say it out loud. She looked down at the table. '. . . to Kimberley,' she muttered.

Anton flung himself backwards on the bench and whooped with laughter.

'To Kimberley, hey?' He slapped the table. 'Are you sure we can't take you to Timbuktu, while we're at it?'

Rifke reddened. Again. She didn't know how to respond. She glanced over at Mevrou van Niel, who was frowning.

'Listen here, girlie,' Anton said. He tapped her arm. She looked up at him. 'We won't be driving you anywhere.' He smiled. His teeth were toothpaste-advert white, slightly crossed in the front.

'But –' she started to say. Anton laid his hand on her arm for a moment. I need to get to Kimberley, she continued in her head.

'We won't be driving you anywhere because we doesn't – don't – have any vehicles that work. No truck. No car. Not even a tractor. It is because of the War. No petrol. Not round here anyway. And even with petrol, girlie, the vehicles is . . . broken . . . don't work.'

Rifke felt a chill creep across her scalp. Her heart raced. How the hell was she going to get away?

'What about . . . what about the other people round here? Neighbours. They – someone must have—'

Anton cut her short with a wave. 'There is no one left in this area since the Cilliers moved away. No one for about a hundred and fifty, two hundred miles.'

Rifke's chest tightened. There had to be some way out. The train. Of course! She'd arrived by train. She'd leave by train.

'I – When's the next – Do you have a train timetable? I'll – I can walk back to the station. Take the next train.'

116

'The next train?' Anton smiled again. 'The next train is not coming for one month. Am I right, Mother?'

Mevrou van Niel nodded, her fingers still moving over the sock waiting to be darned.

Anton folded his arms and leaned on the table.

No train for a month? A whole month? Rifke leaped to her feet. She was breathing quickly. 'Uncle Ber – I'll phone him. He'll come. He'll come for me.'

'I'm sorry, girlie.' Anton shook his head, and grinned. 'Driemieliesfontein is still waiting for the wires. We isn't connected yet to the telephone *dingis* . . . whatsername.'

A huge, yawning chasm split open in Rifke's stomach.

'What?' She grabbed hold of the edge of the table for support. She swallowed. Sweat bloomed all over her, yet she felt ice cold. 'I – I – You mean –'

No transport. No neighbours. No train. No phone. Rifke turned to Mevrou van Niel. There must be something she could do. But Mevrou's face was closed.

'Sit.' Anton took Rifke's arm and pulled her down to the bench. 'You has – have – gone very white.' He laughed. 'It is not that bad here.'

His words were a roar in Rifke's ears. The room began to swirl. Bits of it were blotted out. The last thing she remembered was the back of her neck being grabbed and shoved between her knees.

Chapter Eighteen

'Ma?' The murmuring of Ma's prayers made Rifke stir. She opened her eyes. She wasn't on their soft bed with the sag in the middle. And Ma's broad back wasn't leaning into Rifke's drawn-up knees. Rifke was on a hard, narrow bed in a small, bare room. There was a wet rag across her forehead. And Ma was not there.

'*Goed. Jy's beter.*' Mevrou van Niel's face loomed over Rifke, green eyes in a white face. 'You is better.' She spoke slowly. 'I must go now.' She stood up straight. A row of socks she'd been darning hung out of a pocket in her skirt. Rifke blinked, focused on Mevrou van Niel's long bony hands, which kept moving even after she re-threaded the needle through the cloth of her shirt. '*Ek* – I – will in the kitchen be.' She moved to the door, then stopped for a second. She seemed to be about to say something else, but changed her mind and left the room.

Rifke listened to the knock and scuff of her boots against the wooden floor, fading as she made her way down the house. When Ma got up at five every morning, it was exactly that sound that woke Rifke and drove her crazy. Ma's sturdy synagogue shoes, the ones she'd travelled to and from Kimberley in, were the only ones that hadn't had their backs crushed. Rifke felt a sting of that irritation now, tinged with panic and a sense of desolation.

'Red dress,' Rifke said out loud.

That was enough to stifle any guilt before it could take breath. After all, it was Ma's fault she was here. And – it came back to her with a sickening jolt – not just here, but *stranded* here for a whole month.

She looked around. The walls of the room were white. Roughly plastered. Cracked in places. No ceiling, just the thatched roof, patched with ragged pieces of blue sky. But what time was it? Four o'clock? Five maybe? There was a window to the right of the bed, a couple of pigeons on the ledge. It was their murmuring she'd mistaken for Ma's prayers. One of them tipped forward and squirted kak on to a crusted heap on the sill. It made her feel queasy.

As she turned away, her eyes caught on a small wooden cross on the wall above the bed. Jesus sagged off it. Ma would have a lot to say about *Yoske* hovering above Rifke's head. There'd be tutting and finger wagging and puffing and Ma would have bustled on to the bed and yanked the crucifix off the wall. It made Rifke smile to think of it. But she also felt strange and uncomfortable – she, who'd never even stepped into a church, was lying here now, and presumably would be for thirty nights, making herself available for Jesus's protection. It didn't feel right. It seemed fraudulent. And yet, Rifke thought, her head still hurting and her limbs heavy, surely she needed all the protection she could get? She closed her eyes.

When she opened them again, the scraps of sky she could see through the thatch were blue-black. The pigeons had gone. The room was dark. A smell of roasting meat drifted in. Rifke's stomach growled. When had she last eaten? It must have been that chocolate she'd bought at Johannesburg station. She took the rag off her forehead and slowly swung her legs to the side of the bed.

What day was it? They'd arrived in Kimberley on Tuesday and left on the Wednesday evening. Yesterday was Thursday. She'd spent last night on the train . . . which meant that it was Friday. Rifke rubbed her eyes with the heels of her hands. She'd only ever spent Friday night with Ma, or Uncle and Aunty and Mirele. The first stars on a Friday evening ushered in the Sabbath, which would last until the end of the next day.

Rifke looked down at her dress. Even in the dark she could see that it was stained and bedraggled. Ripped too, where that dog had snagged it with his claws. She tried to draw her fingers through her hair, but gave up when they caught in the snarls. Friday evening. She should be in her lemon-yellow skirt and white blouse, her hair freshly washed, and Ma in her green dress and her hair coiled into the hairnet with the sparkles. Rifke sighed. She slipped off the bed and stood up. Someone had taken her shoes off and put them away somewhere. She shuffled towards the door in her socks and felt and sniffed her way down a long passage.

The kitchen was the only lit room in the house: candlelight made dancing shadows on the walls. Rifke stood for a moment in the doorway.

'Um . . .' she said, and tapped on the door. 'Er . . . good evening.'

The faces at the table looked otherworldly in the candles' glow. They turned to look at her. It took a moment or two for Rifke to recognize Piet and Hendrik and Anton. There was another boy at the table too – a boy she hadn't yet seen, a bit younger than Anton, Rifke guessed. Shaggy-haired and thin in the face. Clearly another of Mevrou van Niel's sons. No sign of the caramel-coloured baby though. Or the woman she'd heard shouting from inside the outbuilding – the maid, perhaps, off duty that evening. Mevrou herself stood at one end of the table, her sleeves rolled up, slicing a joint of meat.

'*Ja*,' she said and nodded quickly at Rifke. 'Sit.'

Rifke made for the nearest empty chair and slid on to it. There was a gasp from one of the younger boys. Too late, Rifke realized she'd sat in someone's special seat. Meneer van Niel's perhaps. She felt her face heat up and quickly got to her feet, her eyes sweeping the table for another place. The boy she hadn't seen before shifted to make space on the bench between himself and Anton.

'Not so quick, Willem,' Anton muttered. He turned

his back on his brother. 'You sit here, girlie,' he said more loudly. He moved up on the bench so Rifke could sit on the edge, next to him. He smiled, and his teeth and eyes gleamed in the candlelight. 'Now,' he said, and rested a heavy hand on Rifke's shoulder for a moment, 'you's looking much, much better. So you can now tell us your name.'

Mevrou van Niel stopped in mid-slice. Everyone waited for Rifke to speak. She cleared her throat.

'My name is Rif– Rebecca,' she said.

Why had she given the English version of her name? she wondered, surprised at herself.

She touched some tangled strands of hair at her temple. Was it such a terrible thing anyway? After all, she'd tried to tell those English twins in Kimberley her real name and they hadn't understood it. And Mirele had called herself Miriam.

She tossed her head. 'Rebecca,' she said again, firmly. Saying it a second time made it more hers.

'Pass to Rebecca, please, Anton,' Mevrou van Niel said, handing a white plate across the table. On it were two thick slices of meat, a mound of mashed potato and four or five discs of boiled carrot, like spilled coins. Mevrou served herself last. She bent her head, and her children copied her. She spoke her thanks in slow Afrikaans, giving each word equal weight. The light bounced off their five blond heads.

Rifke looked around the table. Bread, but no wine.

Never mind. She closed her eyes and rattled off the Friday-night prayers in her mind, blessing the candles and the bread. She finished just as Mevrou van Niel did. There was a moment's silence as Mevrou looked at the seat Rifke had mistakenly taken. Mevrou then put her hands together and bent her head again. Was she praying for Meneer van Niel?

Piet and Hendrik held their knives and forks up in readiness for their mother's signal. And when she nodded, all the boys tucked into their food with gusto. Hungry as she was, Rifke held her cutlery at the side of her plate, paralysed. Meat. Its smell was unfamiliar. Not lamb, not beef. There were bristles poking through the crusty layer of fat that circled the pale pink inside. *Gebrotn khazerl.* Not only unkosher, but pork-unkosher. Rifke broke out in a sweat. Around her everyone was eating. Rifke lifted her fork. She put it down again. If she weren't going to eat the meat, she should say so now. It shouldn't be wasted. But how could she refuse the meat without offending Mevrou van Niel?

'You feeling sick?' Anton asked, jerking his head at her plate.

'Er . . . yes . . . no . . . I just can't eat the meat. I can't eat pork.'

'You cannot the meat eat?' Mevrou asked. She was frowning. Everyone stopped eating. There was a sudden silence. One of the candles guttered.

'No – er, it's . . . because I am Jewish,' Rifke stammered.

'*Wat bedoel* "Jewish", Anton?' Mevrou van Niel asked.

'*Jood*, Moeder,' Willem said, before Anton could reply. His voice was low. It was the first time Rifke had heard him speak.

Piet and Hendrik whispered the word '*Jood*' between them. Mevrou van Niel looked at Rifke, the candlelight carving deeper hollows in her face.

'I have not met a . . . a Jewish before,' Mevrou van Niel said. Her face showed no emotion. She held out her hand. 'Pass your plate, Rebecca.' With a knife and one sharp movement she wiped the meat off Rifke's plate and on to the carving board, and passed the plate back.

'Thank you. S-sorry,' Rifke said. Not wanting to antagonize Mevrou van Niel any further, Rifke bent over the plate and took up her cutlery again. She ate the vegetables, careful not to pick up any bits that had dipped their toes in the pool of pork gravy. And still hungry when she'd finished, she promised herself a chunk of polony before she went to sleep.

Chapter Nineteen

Despite the strange bed and the unfamiliar surroundings, Rifke plunged into sleep. She was woken by an animal's shriek that rang out raw and broken in the air – a haunting sound that quivered at a high pitch and was abruptly silenced.

Rifke lay rigid in the hard bed, panic stabbing her stomach. She was still here in the *bundu*. And for a whole month. Hot tears spilled down the sides of her face. 'I want – I want . . .' she said out loud. Aunty's soft face and her gentle pleading eyes swam into her mind, and she yearned for Aunty's plump hands to wipe her tears with her embroidered hankie. 'Oh, Aunty . . .' she cried, and buried her head in the bedlinen. "Rifke, Rifkele,' she knew Aunty would say. 'Perhaps it won't be so bad. One month. It will soon go by . . .'

She rubbed her cheeks on the pillowcase and shifted about between the starchy sheets, which chafed against the sore on her knee and the scratches down her leg. Her hair was still tangled and stiff with grime. But at least the rest of her was clean – Anton had carried a copper pot of hot water into her room after dinner, and she'd sponged herself down before putting on the nightdress Mevrou van Niel had hooked on to the doorknob.

She got out of bed, the nightdress puddling round her feet. The strong beam of sunlight coming through the window and the holes in the thatch suggested it was late morning. Sounds of activity drifted into the room: chickens, cows, the baby crying and a repeated hammering sound. The dog was barking too. It sounded far away, outside somewhere. Thank goodness.

She looked around for her clothes. They'd been removed. Hoping she wouldn't run into any of the boys, she hoisted up the nightdress a little so she could walk more easily and made her way down the passage. It was lighter inside than yesterday, or perhaps she was beginning to get used to the dark interior.

'*Goeie*– er . . . good morning, Rebecca.' It was Willem. He was lugging a heavy metal box out of one of the rooms off the corridor. He seemed almost as embarrassed by her nightclothes as she was; his eyes skimmed the stiff white nightdress and looked away, a mottled blush spreading from his collar upwards.

'Morning,' Rifke said after a second's failure to recognize the name he'd used. She hunched her shoulders and shrunk a little against the wall.

'Er . . .' Willem seemed to be searching for something to say. He was wearing glasses. She hadn't noticed them the evening before. They looked as though he'd had trouble winding them round his face – their wire rims were bent and twisted and one of the lenses had been secured to the frame with a sticking plaster.

'Um . . . I . . . Do you know where your mother is?' Rifke asked.

'*Ja*, yes, I mean. She is doing the washing.' His glasses slid down his nose and he hunched up his shoulder, trying to push them back. His fair hair flopped behind the lenses and into his eyes. 'She is outside, I think.' He was all angles – pointy elbowed, sharp-chinned and bony-kneed. His shirt was loose and his khaki shorts looked flappy over his skinny legs. A *langerloksh*, Ma would have said, a long noodle. Rifke thought he didn't look strong enough to carry the box he was holding.

She was desperate to find her clothes. 'Can you show me . . .'

'Morning, Rebecca.' Anton appeared from nowhere, his bare feet silent on the floorboards. He stepped in front of Willem. There was a rush and clunk of metal against metal – the stuff in the box moving suddenly about. Was it her imagination, or did one of them shove the other? Was it Willem?

'Come with me,' Anton said, smiling down at Rifke. His arm reached across her back and, grasping her elbow, he swept her forward. He smelt of fresh washing, and his arm was hot against Rifke's back, like Atticus's fur when he'd been out in the sun. Everything about this boy was bright and golden. When she glanced back, Willem was following them, his face creased into a scowl.

They had to skirt past the crate, which had been

brought into the kitchen and partially opened. This time Rifke was careful not to graze herself on it.

'My mother, she is in the laundry, Rebecca. Just through that door.' Anton pointed to the corner of the kitchen, his gaze drifting over Rifke's nightdress. 'Nice pyjama,' he said. She blushed. 'I must go now,' he smiled. 'My girls are waiting for me. Udders bursting with milk.' He wandered out of the kitchen, ignoring Willem, who'd begun to lever more of the panels off the crate, using tools from the box he'd carried in.

Rifke opened the door Anton had pointed to. The laundry was a narrow room. Like her bedroom, the walls were roughly plastered and whitewashed. Mevrou van Niel was standing over a heap of crumpled clothing, her head bowed and her large hands covering her face. Light sifted in from a window and created an aura around her. In her beige shirt, long brown skirt and white apron, with her hair tightly coiled into a bun, she looked like someone in an Old Master painting. Unaware of Rifke standing there, she took her hands away from her face and lifted her head to look through the window at the sky.

'*Genadige Vader . . .*' she prayed.

Rifke took a step backwards and turned quietly on her toes so as not to disturb her.

Meanwhile, Willem had dismantled one side of the crate and begun to set its contents out on the table. Rifke saw bags of flour, salt, sugar, rice and mielie meal. There were piles of Sunlight soap bricks and bottles of sham-

poo, rows of assorted medicines in dark brown and blue bottles and rolls of bandages and cotton wool. Inside the crate were neatly stacked bolts of fabric, small reels of sewing thread and bundles of knitting wool speared with knitting needles. Folded clothes and shoes. Books, paper, newspapers. Oil, paraffin and candles. And several other packages Rifke couldn't identify.

Mevrou came up behind Rifke.

'Hello . . . er, good morning,' Rifke said.

'*Goeiedag*,' Mevrou replied, her fingers worrying at a button on her shirt. She didn't smile. Despite the clatter of her boots, there was a silence about her, a remoteness that Rifke had never met in anyone before. She moved past, her skirt brushing Rifke's nightdress.

'I've checked thoroughly, Moeder, and you were right. There are no letters from Pa this time. Usually Aunt Annet puts them right at the top.'

It took Rifke a few seconds to understand what Willem was saying. 'But when you opened the crate, you must have missed this. It's a letter from Aunt Annet.' He held it out to his mother.

'Yes, thank you, Willem. I didn't see it,' Mevrou van Niel said. She took it from him and perched on the edge of the table as she slit open the envelope, her eyes moving quickly over the loose handwriting. Willem went to stand next to her.

Rifke felt like an intruder. She wished she were not

there. But she didn't want to draw attention to herself by moving.

Mevrou van Niel drew herself upright and squared her shoulders. 'So Pa's unit is in Italy. Annet doesn't know any more than that.' She rested her hand on Willem's back, the rustling of the paper in her trembling fingers belying the steady calm of her voice. 'No news is good news.'

So Meneer van Niel had gone off to fight in the War.

Rifke must have made a sound or a movement, because both Willem and his mother turned to look at her. For a moment, neither seemed to register who she was. Then Mevrou van Niel rose. Her hands folded the letter and slotted it back into its envelope and into her apron pocket.

'Rebecca,' she said, 'I have your clothes washed, and on the line hanged.' She seemed to take in the hugeness of her nightdress on Rifke's small frame. Rifke thought she saw a softening around her eyes, a hint of humour perhaps, although it vanished quickly without reaching any other part of her face. 'For . . . a little time, you must wear my sons' clothes. *Wag* . . . wait a bittie. I shall them to you bring.' She made her way back into the laundry.

Willem meanwhile carried on taking stuff out of the crate. He unwrapped a huge pair of scissors and placed them on the table next to other sewing bits and pieces. The brown paper they'd been wrapped in he smoothed and folded, taking care to line up the corners. He glanced at Rifke and looked away immediately, half turning his back to her. Rude. What had she done to offend him?

'Rebecca. *Kom* . . . come.' Mevrou van Niel reappeared, carrying a pile of clothing.

'Thank you,' Rifke said.

She followed her long, straight back out of the kitchen and down the corridor towards her room. Mevrou laid the clothes out on the bed: a cotton shirt with ghosted checks, a pair of trousers, patched in places. Ma would have something to say about those. Women were not supposed to wear men's clothes.

Mevrou placed a pair of socks alongside the trousers. Then, for a moment she hesitated, her hands for once still, a faint flush on her cheeks. She drew from her apron pocket two folded pieces of fabric, white against her reddened knuckles, lace-edged and suddenly frivolous next to the austere masculine clothes.

'I do not think the fit is *goed* . . . good, but it is all that I has.' She placed the white things on the bed next to the socks and turned to leave.

'*Baie dankie*, Mevrou. Thank you,' Rifke said, feeling herself blush too.

Mevrou van Niel nodded and shut the door behind her.

Chapter Twenty

Shortly after Rifke's thirteenth birthday, Ma had taken her to two Lithuanian dressmakers. They had created a brassiere for Rifke out of a grown-up's huge foundation garment. She'd had to stand under a stark light – her face bright red and an embarrassing amount of sweat trickling from her armpits – while they pinned the hefty fabric around her chest. The brassiere Mevrou van Niel had left for her was similarly enormous. Perhaps she'd starched it: it was stiff and it crackled, and no matter how many times Rifke tried to flatten it, the fabric sprang into two rigid cones.

The knickers, while not overly loose round the waist, were very long. Down to her knees, in fact. And when Rifke pulled the trousers on, the knickers rucked up into ridges around the top of her legs. She twitched at them to straighten them out, but it still felt as though she were wearing two pairs of trousers.

'I can't. I just can't wear these things,' she muttered, striding up and down the room, trying to walk normally and at the same time pummelling the brassiere to make it flat. She felt embarrassed and cross and uncomfortable. She knew she should be grateful, but that just made her more bad-tempered.

'That's it.' She stopped pacing. 'I'm taking this damn thing off for a start.' Unhooking the brassiere at the back, she withdrew her arms from its stiff straps and pulled the undergarment through the shirtsleeves. She flung it on the bed and marched out to collect her own one.

She found her way to the French windows that led to the back garden. Through the doors Rifke could see her clothes hanging on the line. She blushed. Any of the boys might have seen her underwear. Another reason to rush out and grab it. She turned the doorknob. The dog leaped up from the shadows. Chained to the post, it lunged towards the house, its throttled gasps loud even through the glass. Rifke slammed the door shut. It couldn't reach her. She knew that, but she still felt nervous.

She waited a moment, watching as the dog began to give up. The side gate whined and the baby pottered into the garden, his auburn head bobbing from side to side. Rifke was happy to see him again.

'Hello, little one,' she called. 'Where've you sprung from?'

The baby seemed surprised to see her. He stared at her as if trying to place her. Then with a smile he dropped the toy he'd been carrying and moved towards something lying on the ground. The dog's half-chewed bone.

'No!' Rifke screamed. She burst through the door just as the dog leaped. 'Don't you dare hurt him!' Seizing the baby by the wrist, she yanked him towards her, lifted him on to her hip and ran back inside the house. Behind them the dog was baying. The baby stared at Rifke for a moment, then he opened his mouth as wide as an oven door and let out a howl.

'Shh, shh, baby. It's all right now,' she said, as much to reassure herself as him. She joggled him about on her hip as she'd seen Farieda do with her granddaughter. But it just made his wails more wobbly.

'Shh, shh,' she tried again. Was it delayed shock or was he screaming because he hadn't been able to have the bone? Was his mother anywhere? Rifke looked through the French windows, but there was no sign of anyone outside. She moved down the passage, the baby's arms clasped around her neck and his bawling mouth right next to her ear.

'Come on, let's go and see what Mevrou van Niel has in the kitchen, shall we?'

The kitchen was empty. Willem had gone, and the crate had been removed. Some of the stuff that had been packed inside it had been left on the table. Above the baby's crying, Rifke could just hear the familiar scuff and knock of boots coming from the laundry. She was relieved when Mevrou emerged, an empty basket tucked under her arm. She'd definitely know what to do.

'Oh, Mevrou.' Rifke had to shout to make herself heard. 'I can't stop him crying. Do you . . .'

To her surprise, Mevrou turned her head away, the

cords in her neck standing proud. She pressed the basket closer to her side and walked out.

Rifke frowned, confused.

Meanwhile, the baby's cries were shrill and insistent. Rifke paced up and down the kitchen. What could she distract him with? There was no food around, and even if there had been, she wouldn't dare give him something that wasn't hers. She'd take him back to the outbuilding she'd seen him go into the day before.

'Let's go, baby,' she said. He was quietening down now. He nestled closer into Rifke's neck and nuzzled her. It felt a bit tickly. But cosy too. Comforting. He must just have been bathed; he smelt of soap and his hair was damp against Rifke's skin.

Avoiding the back garden – the dog's lair – Rifke found her way to the entrance hall. She recognized the front door by the mosaic of light coming from the big many-paned window she'd seen above it. The door handle was stiff and groaned from disuse when she twisted it. Still, the door opened, and Rifke picked her way down the front path and across to the outbuildings. The baby took hold of her hair and held it in his fist while he sucked his thumb.

The door to the outbuilding he'd entered the day before was ajar. Rifke stood for a moment on the threshold.

'Hello?' she called, and tapped on the door.

It swung open. The smell of woodsmoke and earth

and something yeasty – something that stirred a memory – filled her nose. Rifke stepped into the room. The floor was clay or dung, the walls soot-blackened. A three-legged metal pot balanced on top of a small fire in the middle of the room. The room felt cold despite it. She hugged herself and looked around wide-eyed. Grass mats and animal skins were strewn about. Blankets were stacked on the floor, and there were strings of beads and dried furry, leathery things hanging on the wall. Clay pots with woven grass lids huddled together in front of a platform at the back of the room. Sticks and carved wooden implements and stones were set out in rows on the floor. There was a book in the school library about the tribes of southern Africa, and this was like one of the photos of the inside of a native person's hut.

The sound of water splashing against tin came from the garden. Perhaps the boy's mother was out there doing the washing. Or having a bath.

'Hello! I've got your son here,' Rifke called more loudly.

Through the doorway at the other end of the room she could see a slice of the garden at the back of the out-building. Someone was cultivating some sort of crop: green leaves sprouted from the soil at regular intervals.

She shifted the baby on her hip. He was asleep now, his breath buzzing against her neck. There were no beds and she cast about for a soft place to lay him down.

'O-oh!' she gasped. What *was* that? She tiptoed closer.

A goat lying across a stone in the corner. Its belly slit. An empty pelt. Eyes open, no longer glassy, but cloudy, the minus signs in their centres still visible. Flies lining the rims like kohl. And the knife that had slit its body lying next to it. It didn't smell, or if it did she couldn't smell it above the stronger smells in the room. Stepping backwards quickly, she held the baby more tightly. How could someone leave a knife lying there with a small child running around?

Then the hairs on her arms stiffened. She stood suddenly still. She was being watched.

Chapter Twenty-One

A black girl of about sixteen or seventeen stood behind Rifke. It was as if she'd just materialized in the room, but Rifke could see wet footprints leading inside to where she stood.

The girl was slightly built, swamped by the orange blanket wrapped around her body and under her arms. For a second she stared at Rifke, startled. Her eyes were wide and black, pupil-less it seemed, and crazed. Then she sprang forward with slick grace. As the girl grabbed the sleeping boy, water from her many long plaits sprayed Rifke's face and she trod on Rifke's toes.

Rifke's body immediately began to chill in the places where the baby had been lying. She hunched her shoulders and crossed her arms around her chest. The girl backed away, her eyes still fixed on Rifke's. The baby, crushed against the girl's chest, jerked awake and made stuttering noises.

'I – I was just bringing him back,' Rifke said, still alarmed. But then she thought of the dog, and the naked knife with its cruel curve, and she felt a surge of anger.

'You know, I found him near that vicious dog,' she said. 'I got him just in time – just before the dog went for him.'

The girl glared at Rifke, her eyebrows arched high into her forehead. Metal glinted from the objects plugging the huge holes in her earlobes.

'The dog – you know –' Rifke felt for the Afrikaans word – '*die hond* was going to bite him.'

Still the girl said nothing, and Rifke didn't know if she'd understood her, but in her silence and the tightening of her fists across the baby's back Rifke sensed she shouldn't remain there. She shivered, glad for the first time of the big shirt and trousers she was wearing. She made for the door, not looking at the girl but still aware of her stare. Her toes were stinging where the girl had trodden on them. Something made her turn round as she stepped outside. The girl was in the doorway. One arm was raised, as though about to hurl a stone, but her hand, curled slightly, was empty. She said something in a language Rifke didn't recognize, her voice starting low before rising to a shriek.

Warning or curse? Rifke wasn't waiting around to find out. She lowered her head and darted down the path away from the outbuilding, sand spraying beneath her feet. Tears blinded her.

How was she going to stay here for a whole month?

'You must take no notice of Izula.'

Anton had appeared at her side. Rifke stopped and quickly wiped her nose on her shoulder. Anton laughed. He was wearing shorts and holding his balled-up shirt in his hand. His hair was wet; so was his chest. The beaded choker around his neck was wet too. He fingered it a moment, then rubbed himself dry with the crumpled shirt. 'She believes she is a . . . a wizard, I think you call it. Look!' He nudged Rifke to make her turn around. 'Look at her now!'

The girl was bent over, holding the baby with one arm, scooping at something on the ground with her other hand.

'What's she doing?' Rifke asked.

'She is busy collecting the sand from your footprints.'

Rifke looked up at him. He was rubbing dry the tufts of fair hair in his armpits. He paused for a minute.

'*Ja*, Rebecca.' He smiled. 'It is true.'

'But what for? Why would she do that?'

He put his shirt on before answering. 'She will use it to make medicine. So she can – what is the words – put spells on you.' He turned and waggled his fingers near Rifke's face.

'No!' Rifke drew back, incredulous. 'But why *my* footprints? I didn't do anything to her. I was just bringing her brother back.'

'Sibu is not her brother. He is her son.' Anton looked away.

'Her son?'

'*Ja . . . ja* . . . well, I suppose they . . . er . . . start young in her culture.' He sawed at the back of his neck with the side of his hand. '*Ag*, all that magic and spells, it is all rubbish anyway. Nonsense.'

Rifke looked over her shoulder again at the girl Anton had called Izula. She was upright now, watching them as they walked away. 'What has she got against me?' Rifke asked again. 'I wasn't hurting her baby . . . Sibu.'

Anton bent to break off a stalk of grass, which he slid between his teeth. He seemed not to have heard her.

They had almost reached the front door of the main house when Anton stopped and flung his arm out across the front of Rifke's body.

'Ow!' she shouted.

'Shh!' Anton put a finger to his lips. He dropped down and crouched at Rifke's feet, and in one swooping movement he picked up a stone between his thumb and forefinger and flung it. It opened out into a straight line as it left his hand, then turned into an undulating scribble in mid-air. It landed far down the drive, a dark mark on the ground, still for a second or two, then a quicksilver slither off into the trees.

'What . . . ?'

'Puff adder. Baby one,' Anton said. 'Maybe Izula is already making her spells.'

Flinging his head back, he laughed as he opened the front door for Rifke. He placed his hand against her back for a second, then sauntered off, raking his fingers through his hair. 'You should better always wear boots round here!' he called over his shoulder.

A puff adder? Rifke shuddered and took a couple of deep breaths. She'd been within an inch of a snake, a really venomous snake, one of the most dangerous snakes in South Africa. What if she'd stepped on it? She shut the front door behind her and ran through the cool of the house to the kitchen.

Willem was there, packing stuff away in the cupboards. He turned to look at Rifke.

'What has happened? Your face is white.' He came over to her. 'Quick. Sit down.'

Rifke subsided on to the bench. Trembling, she put her hands to her face. 'I – I . . . nearly trod on a puff adder.'

'Are you all right?' He sat next to her, looking at her, concerned.

She nodded. 'Yes. Anton saved me.' She thought of how he'd picked up the snake. How he'd seemed like Moses holding out the rod that had turned into a serpent. 'He saved my life,' she said. She thought of that savage dog on her arrival. 'Again,' she added.

'*Ag.*' Willem made an impatient noise and got up off the bench. His face was back to its normal scowl. '*Ja,* well, he probably planted that snake there so that it would look like he was saving you,' he muttered. He stood for a minute in front of her. '*Pas op*, Rebecca,' his voice louder now. 'Be careful. Anton is danger—'

'What are you speaking about, Willem?' Mevrou van Niel had walked in. She spoke to him in Afrikaans. A bucket full of soil-encrusted potatoes and carrots hung from one hand, while her other hand was smoothing the surface of an onion.

'*Niks nie*, Moeder. Nothing.' Willem cast a glance at Rifke as he took the bucket from his mother.

Rifke frowned. Why had he said those things about Anton? Was Willem jealous of his brother? Rifke heard an echo of Ma's voice – 'Just jealous,' she'd said when Rifke had told her some girls at school had been whispering about her.

Mevrou glanced at the shirt and trousers Rifke was wearing. Her eyes fell on Rebecca's bare feet, dusted with red earth. 'Oh . . . you hasn't put on the boots. I left them there by your door. Rebecca, here it is *baie* – very . . .' she turned to Willem for the English word.

'Dangerous. Very dangerous,' he said, looking at Rifke, his eyes dark behind his glasses.

Chapter Twenty-Two

'I met the black girl . . . Izula. I met her this morning,' Rifke said. She was standing in the middle of the kitchen, while Mevrou van Niel prepared the dinner. Mevrou had said nothing, only shaken her head, when Rifke had offered to help her in the kitchen that afternoon. She felt uncomfortable. In Johannesburg, Ma had never allowed her to be idle, and in the background there'd always been the traffic, the Leibowitzes' gramophone and Ma's endless prayers.

The rhythm of Mevrou's knife hitting the chopping board altered for a split second. Although she didn't say anything, Rifke was sure she'd heard her.

Quite apart from the silence in the kitchen, Rifke's encounter with the girl had unsettled her; she felt uneasy – not sure whether she should be worried about the spells Anton had mentioned, or whether he was just teasing her – and she was curious.

'Who is she – Izula, I mean?' Rifke tried again.

The chopping stopped. Mevrou van Niel's back stiffened. She shifted her feet in their boots, tapped the onion half she was holding with her left forefinger.

'Izula . . . one day she comes here,' she said eventually. 'With two goats. We doesn't know where she comes

from.' Her voice was cold. 'We think from far away. Zululand, *miskien* – maybe.' She took up the knife again.

How strange, Rifke thought. How strange that she and Izula should both wash up in Driemieliesfontein like bits of driftwood. Had Izula's turning up out of the blue made her own appearance less of a shock? It was odd, the way none of the Van Niels seemed interested in where she'd come from or the kind of life she'd led. Perhaps it was shyness.

And what about Sibu? Had he come with Izula? And what was Izula's role anyway? In the short time Rifke'd had been at the farm, it had been Mevrou van Niel whom she'd seen washing and sorting laundry, ironing, collecting vegetables, cooking the food and sweeping the floors. If Izula were not a maid, was she perhaps a farmhand?

'Does she work here?' Rifke persisted.

This time the rhythm of Mevrou's chopping didn't alter. When she turned to scrape the onions into a pot, Rifke could see from the set of her mouth that the subject was closed.

Chapter Twenty-Three

Darkness fell before they'd finished dinner that evening. Willem lit the lanterns on the windowsill and on the floor beside the door before lighting the candles on the table. They guttered a little before becoming steady. Piet and Hendrik hadn't yet got used to having Rifke there. The candlelight played tricks with their faces, as they stared at her when they thought she wasn't looking and looked down at their plates when they saw her staring back at them.

When Mevrou van Niel stood to gather the plates, Rifke stood too. She put out her hands to take them from her.

'Let me –' she said.

Mevrou van Niel made a double click sound: 'Tut-tut.' She shook her head and carried the dishes to the sink.

Rifke brought her hands slowly to her sides. She fumbled at the ridges the foreign knickers made under the trousers she wasn't yet used to. She was aware of all the boys' eyes on her. Anton's eyes especially. How foolish she must look, just standing there. Now, to top it all, she needed the lavatory. And the outhouse wasn't a place you went to until you really had to – especially not after dark. Rifke had spotted a chipped porcelain potty under her bed. Just the thought of carrying that out in the morning made her shudder. It was better to make the journey outside before she went to sleep.

'Please, Mevrou, I need . . .' She spoke in English. Her Afrikaans had deserted her.

Mevrou van Niel turned from the sink and looked at her blankly.

'I need to go . . . outside,' Rifke said, heat gathering at her collar. 'May I take a lantern?'

Mevrou wiped her hands on her apron. She leaned across to the windowsill and lifted the lantern down. She passed it to Rifke, the light drawing heavy lines under her eyes.

'Do you want I should go with you?' Anton asked. Unlike his brothers, the candlelight just made him look even more golden.

Willem snorted.

Piet whispered something to Hendrik. Rifke heard the words '*pas op vir die slang in die toilet*' – watch out for the snake in the toilet – and both boys giggled.

So Willem had told them about the puff adder. And now they were mocking her, were they?

Rifke shook her head. 'No. No, thank you,' she said to Anton. She didn't want them to think she was completely lily-livered. Besides, how could she possibly use the lavatory with Anton hovering outside?

She took the lantern and made her way down the

passage to the side door – well away from the dog – that opened on to the side of the house. A wind had come up. The dry bushes along the sandy track leading up to the outhouse tossed and clawed at her as she passed. The lantern light elongated the shadows. Everything looked misshapen. Every stone was a coiled snake until it scattered from under her boots.

There was barely enough room in the shack for her and the lantern, but she wasn't going in there without it. Holding her breath, she checked every corner. Inside the lavatory too. It smelt almost as thick as it had during the day.

Breathing through her mouth, Rifke lowered herself on to the wooden seat. At that moment she would even have preferred to squat behind the big tree in Joubert Park. If she went to the lavatory on average six times a day, that would make about one hundred and eighty visits in her month here. Too many to think about.

But at least someone had tidied up in there since her last visit. The brown wrapping paper from the stuff in the crate had been cut into neat squares, a hole punched in the corner of each, and tied together with string. They hung off a nail. The posters of Judy Garland and the other film stars that had beamed down at her on previous visits were now covered with the October, November and December pages of last year's calendar.

Rifke stared at the days not long past. She would have been in Johannesburg then, at school, visiting Ruthie,

buying chickens at Mrs Kossoff's. She needed to mark off her time at Driemieliesfontein. The new calendar she'd seen in the crate was now hanging on the laundry door. She'd ask Mevrou for a piece of paper and a pen so she could copy it out.

In films, days peeled off the calendar, flying away like leaves in a storm. Mevrou's calendar was a sturdier affair, one page per month, each sponsored by a Johannesburg business. January was John Orr's. Ma had taken Rifke to their local branch for pyjamas before they'd left for Kimberley. How far away her life in Johannesburg now was.

'Today is Saturday, eighth January,' she said out loud, looking at her handwritten version. She counted off the days until the next train was due. 'Twenty-nine, thirty, thirty-one. That makes it Sunday, sixth February.' She drew a heavy circle around it.

She set her calendar on the table next to her bed, blew out her candle and placed the saucer over the calendar. She was tired. Outside, the leaves rattled in the wind. From down the passage she could hear the hum of Mevrou van Niel's sewing machine. Otherwise the house was quiet. Saturday nearly over. Dov Kossoff would have come round to their flat. Strange that she felt none of the horror she'd felt – when was it? – only two days before, at the thought of his seeing Ma's housecoat and their miserable life. And anyway, images of Anton kept edging Dov Kossoff out. Anton's tanned chest. His crossed white teeth. The cleft in his chin. He'd put his arm around her that morning, rested his hand on her shoulder, on her back. She hugged herself and smiled.

Deep in the night, Rifke's door whined. She snapped open her eyes. Froze. A denser darkness against the doorway. Her scalp prickled, stabbed by a million needles. Someone there. Leaving her room. The light sanding of feet against the wooden floor. The smell of something she couldn't name hanging in the air above her bed.

'Who's there?' she called. 'What do you want?'

She sat up, stiff against her pillows, holding her breath. The footfalls were fading. Had they really gone? Rifke knew she wouldn't be able to sleep unless she checked.

She pushed back the bedclothes and crept to the door. The passage was dark. Still. Silent. She stood for a second, her heartbeat hammering in her ears. Had there really been someone? Could she have dreamed it? What could they have wanted? Her blue canvas bag was her only possession. And it was still there, a dark rectangle hanging off the door handle. She patted her way back to her bed.

To comfort herself, she tried to summon up the elusive man in the cream suit of whom she'd often dreamed. But it was no use. It was like the time the projector had broken down in the cinema – the image appeared, only to judder and fade and disappear into dispersed grey speckles.

Rifke stayed awake the rest of the night. She watched the sun feel its way into her room.

'Rebecca.' Mevrou knocked on her door. 'Today it is *Sondag* – Sunday. We shall now must to prayers go. Your clothes is dry. They is here.'

Chapter Twenty-Four

At first, Rifke tried to concentrate on understanding the prayers Mevrou van Niel was saying. But her head felt thick from lack of sleep, and soon she let the even tones of Mevrou's voice wash over her. They were in some sort of little church or chapel reached through a dark room off the main passage. The room was plain. Whitewashed walls, six straight-backed chairs arranged in a semicircle around a single, larger chair, and a big wooden cross on the wall.

Mevrou van Niel sat in the central chair. She was wearing an ancient straw bonnet, something her Dutch ancestors might have worn a hundred years before. It looked like she had her head in a tunnel. When she turned a page in her bible, her blouse crackled. The boys were in white shirts and dark trousers, Willem's bony wrists six inches from the cuffs. Rifke stared at him. Had it been him in her room? Let him try it again. She'd call for Anton next time.

Anton had kept a chair for Rifke beside him. The cotton of his shirt rustled when he moved and gave off the comforting smell of starch.

What would Ma say about all this – a church – and Rifke sitting there in her yellow dress – the yellow dress

Aunty had sent in September for Rosh Hashanah, the Jewish New Year? Shouting loudly in Yiddish, Ma burst through her thoughts in her stained green housecoat, her face puce with anger and brandishing a wooden spoon.

But even though the image of Ma was so vivid, she appeared in Rifke's mind like a cartoon character – small and unreal. And so very far away. Rifke felt again that freedom she'd felt running through Joubert Park. Anton looked down at her just at that minute and caught Rifke's eye. He held her gaze for a second or two longer than usual, and – of course – Rifke's face caught fire. She bent her head, noticing for the first time the tiny stitches where Mevrou van Niel had repaired the tears in her dress.

The door to the chapel opened slowly. Grateful for a diversion, Rifke turned to see who had come in. Sibu.

Mevrou van Niel paused in her reading. She seemed to look through Sibu, rather than at him. Then she continued. But beneath the bible resting in her hands, Rifke saw Mevrou's fingers worrying at her wedding band.

Sibu had been crying. Tear tracks and snot trails ran in parallel lines down his face. He padded across the room, heading for Mevrou van Niel.

'Sibu!' Willem hissed, and reached for him.

But he swerved and kept on towards Mevrou. Like a cat he eased himself against her. And like a cat he'd chosen the person who was least sympathetic. Mevrou van Niel froze. Then edged away from Sibu, turning her back on him. But not before Sibu had rubbed his face against her, leaving a smudge of snot and red stuff on her skirt. Rifke leaned forward to get a closer look. Blood?

Mevrou van Niel was unaware of the smears and had carried on reading. Sibu moved on to Anton, who stiffened. Mevrou's voice didn't falter. From under his bible, Piet stretched out a hand to Sibu and beckoned.

But it was Rifke who was now the object of Sibu's attentions. She opened her arms and Sibu tottered over to her. She lifted him on to her lap, and he hesitated a moment before wrapping his arms around her. Rifke patted him on the back, then held him away from her to see where he'd hurt himself. She saw at once that there were blobs of fresh blood on his earlobes. They'd been pierced. A thick piece of grass had been stuck into each hole, knotted on either side of the lobe. Blood kept seeping through.

'Look!' Rifke mouthed at Anton, pointing at Sibu's ears.

Anton nodded and turned back to his bible.

He's bleeding! she wanted to shout out loud. But they were all absorbed in Mevrou's reading.

Blood dripped on to Sibu's shoulder. Rifke waited until Mevrou had reached a pause, then, holding Sibu against herself, she tiptoed out of the chapel. Surely Mevrou couldn't object to her helping the child.

*

Rifke found a stack of paper tissues among the bandages and cotton wool Willem had packed away in one of the kitchen cupboards.

'Come, Sibu,' she said, and patted the bench for him to sit down. He looked up at her with his amber eyes. She smiled. 'I won't hurt you.'

Pulling out a few tissues, she wiped his nose and dabbed at his seeping earlobes. He sat very still, saying nothing. 'Do you want a drink of water?' she asked in Afrikaans.

He didn't answer, but she got up anyway to pump some of the ice-cold water into a cup for him. When she turned around, he was running out of the room, a clump of white tissues in his hand. She lingered for a moment. Then Willem lolloped into the room. His face was flushed, unsmiling. Already his shirt was coming untucked.

'Rebecca, do you wish to come with us?' He tossed his head to clear his hair where it was tangled in his glasses. 'After prayers on Sunday, we always pays our respects to the dead.'

'Yes. Thank you,' she said, wondering what he meant.

She replaced the tissue packet in the cupboard and followed Willem down the passage. He moved like a puppet – as if his puppeteer didn't quite have the hang of his strings yet. Ma would have called him a *klutz*.

When he opened the back door, Rifke hung back. She looked to left and right.

'The dog, Leeu, is not here,' Willem said. 'He is now somewhere else chained up.'

Rifke let her breath out slowly. What a relief. How thoughtful of Anton. She made a mental note to thank him.

Willem led Rifke out of the gate and on to the path she'd first taken to get to the house. They turned right as if going towards the barns and animal stalls, but the track divided and continued through an avenue of kaffirbooms. Willem walked alongside Rifke. She was careful not to brush against those gangly, free-ranging arms of his. And she sensed that he was trying to rein them in.

The sun was at its hottest, the sky white with heat. Rifke put her hand to her brow to shield her eyes. Already sweat was blooming in her armpits and down her back. A couple of flies nagged at her, and she flapped at them with her other hand.

'You all right, Rebecca?' he asked. 'The sun . . .'

'Fine. I'm fine.' He didn't need to fuss over her. She lifted her hair from the back of her neck, hoping for a breeze to cool her down.

The rest of the Van Niels were ahead. They were standing in front of some sort of enclosure of whitewashed walls, weathered like the main house and scabbed with bird kak. Mevrou van Niel was having trouble with the high gate. Anton leaned forward and gave it a hefty shake. It didn't budge.

'Willem!' Mevrou called, turning towards Rifke and Willem. '*Daar is iets verkeerd.*'

Rifke understood the Afrikaans – something wrong with the gate.

Willem bent over the gate's catch. His long fingers, like his mother's, moved with surprising grace as he detached a metal spur and manoeuvred something else, and the gate clicked open.

'*Dankie*, Willem.' Mevrou van Niel placed her hand softly on his sleeve, gathering a little of the cotton between her fingers. She may have smiled at him, but Rifke couldn't see past the straw bonnet.

They all shuffled through the gate into the family cemetery. A couple of big trees covered in scented purple flowers threw their branches out over the graves. Rifke stepped into their welcome shade. She wavered. Ma never allowed her to walk beneath a tree with its roots in a graveyard. Something about the tree being fed by the dead. Rifke had never really thought about it, but now an image flashed into her mind of the knuckled roots clawing through the soil and into the decaying coffins. She shivered. The sunlight, when she stepped back into it, was all the more searing. But then surely Ma would prefer her not to get freckles. She took one step back so that she was half in, half out of the shade. Then put a hand to her forehead in disbelief. What was she doing? Some sort of compromise with Ma who wasn't even there?

Mevrou van Niel and all four of her sons were gathered around a grave near to the entrance. A recent burial, judging by the darker colour of the earth. Rifke moved towards them, but hung back beyond their circle, unwilling to intrude.

As the others moved on, Anton broke away from the group. He came to stand next to Rifke.

'Whose grave is this?' Rifke asked. 'Did someone pass away recently?'

'Pa's mother,' Anton said. 'She is in June dead.' He flipped his hair back. '*Ja*, she came from England. It was my great-grandparents, after they came to South Africa from the *Neder*– Netherlands, I think you say – they brought her here to teach English to Oupa *se* . . . Grandfather's young sisters.' He laughed. 'She is ended up marrying Oupa. *Ja*, Rebecca, she thought she was coming for six months.' He nudged the mound of her grave with the tip of his boot. 'And she is here still.' Undoing his top button, he turned to Rebecca. His eyebrows rose and a smile played at his lips as a thought occurred to him. 'You better watch out, Rebecca!'

'Why?' Rebecca hadn't really taken in the last thing he'd said. She'd been watching Mevrou van Niel put a sprig of the purple flowers in a stone jar on the grave. Jewish people put a small stone on the grave to show they'd visited. Strange, how different people had different rituals. Which did she prefer? A flower was prettier than a stone, less sombre, but it would wither soon. The stone would remain, unchanging, until the next visit.

'It could happen to you too – over here for one month you think, but you stay forever!'

Rifke shook her head and smiled.

He looked at the grave again. '*Ja*, Grandma, you was *baie trots* . . . very proud of Pa going to be a soldier on the side of the British. And you must be very, very proud of the English I am speaking to this *skone* . . . beautiful girl from Johannesburg.'

No one had ever called her beautiful. Well, Aunty had, and Uncle Ber, but they didn't count. Rifke looked down and pretended to have found something to pick at on her dress. A shadow fell across her. When she looked up, Willem was standing in front of her and Anton. As usual, he was scowling. What did he want?

The dog barked in the distance. Leeu. Rifke tapped Anton on the arm. 'Thank you, Anton, for taking Leeu away.'

'Taking Leeu away?' Anton looked puzzled.

'Thank you for chaining him up far away from the house. I'm, um . . . really scared of him.'

Anton's frown turned into a broad smile. '*Ja*, I tied him up very good, I promise you.'

Willem made a sound. Like something had caught in his throat. Anton stepped past him and ushered Rifke along.

Mevrou van Niel called Anton and Willem over to

where she was standing. Rifke lingered by the grandmother's grave. Instead of a formal headstone with chiselled lettering, she had a large rock, her name painted on it in black at a slight angle:

Cecily van Niel, nee Wainwright, 1856–1943
Rest in Piece

Rifke wondered how Cecily would have felt about the spelling mistake. Had she been a stiff matriarch who insisted on tea and cucumber sandwiches at four o'clock? Or perhaps a soft English rose, all dimples and twinkles, willing to overlook the misspelling, thrilled that they'd at least taken the trouble to write it in English? Rifke moved on, reading off the names of the generations of van Niels who'd moved, inevitably, from the main house to this enclosure.

Chapter Twenty-Five

On the way out of the cemetery, Rifke noticed a fenced-off section a few hundred feet away, studded with thorn trees and what looked like more graves.

'They is dead slaves,' Anton replied, when Rifke asked. 'Once the Van Niels is having many slaves here at Driemieliesfontein.'

'Slaves? Where did they come from?'

Anton made a vague gesture with his hand. 'Hell, man – now you is asking.' His embarrassed smile was charming.

'Malaysia. They mostly was Malays,' Willem said, overtaking Anton and Rifke. He loped ahead, catching up with Mevrou van Niel and the two younger boys.

'All right, *meneer alles-weet* . . . mister know-everything,' Anton said to his departing back.

Rifke laughed. Sometimes she felt the same way about Mirele. Twenty-eight days to go until the next train. Perhaps it wasn't going to be so bad after all.

Mevrou and the other boys were almost out of sight when Rifke and Anton approached the divide in the path. Rifke heard before she saw them: a bobbing brown-and-grey mass of insistent, ill-tempered goats, smelling of earth. Suddenly Izula rose up in their midst, materializing out of nowhere. She must have been crouching down. Anton and Rifke stopped. The bickering animals passed between them and Izula like a fast-moving, muddy river. Anton fingered his bead necklace. Izula kept her unblinking eyes fixed on him. Beside her, Sibu was darting about in the dust, trying to catch any unsuspecting goat to dab them with the paper tissues still clamped in his fist. Rifke smiled.

Izula took a step forward, causing the last few goats to skitter away. She stabbed the earth with the thick stick in her hand. Her plaits swung and the beads at her neck and wrists rattled.

Anton laughed. A mistake. Izula leaned into him and swept the stick up to within an inch of his temple. Her face knotted in anger, she launched into a diatribe in a language Rifke didn't understand but which Anton seemed to. His face closed, and he shook his head once. Then again. He raised his chin. This only made her angrier, and she flew at him once more, the stick raised this time above her head.

Rifke was startled. What should she do? Should she go and get help?

She was about to turn away when Izula lunged at her. That strangely familiar whiff Rifke had smelt in her room now gusted from her mouth as she shouted at Rifke and waved the stick that she still held high.

Rifke turned and put her hands up to her face to protect herself.

Her arm was grasped, fingers digging into her flesh, dragging her round. Rifke lowered her hands. It wasn't Anton pulling her. Izula's face was right up against hers. So close that Rifke could see the pupils in the girl's eyes – enlarged – and the whites not white but yellow, and blood-shot. And – strangely – tearful too.

The girl shouted again, and Rifke pulled away from her rank breath.

'Leave me!' Rifke shouted. She shook her arm and flailed about, trying to tear herself free from the grasping fingers. With her other hand she shoved the girl away. Izula staggered backwards, losing her footing for a second.

Rubbing her arm, Rifke looked around for Anton. Where was he? He'd been there only a moment before. Now he was nowhere to be seen. Panic quickened her heart. She turned to run, to get away from this crazy girl. Sibu's cry made her stop and look round. Izula was scraping the paper tissues out of his hand. Then with a scream she hurled the shredded bits of tissue at Rifke.

Rifke found her legs were trembling as she ran towards the main house. She glanced over her shoulder once again. Izula was looking in her direction, one hand holding Sibu's, the other brandishing the stick in a jagged rhythm. The goats had massed behind her, and above their bleating Rifke could just make out a high-pitched chant.

She flung herself into the house and pulled the door

firmly to. She stood there a moment, catching her breath. The clatter of plates and cutlery coming from the kitchen reminded her that it was lunchtime. Rifke's hands as she washed them were still shaking after her encounter, and when she took her place at the table, she held them together on her lap to still them.

'Where is Anton?' Mevrou van Niel asked, frowning at his empty place.

Rifke was wondering too. How could he have left her like that? Where had he gone?

'He was walking with me. We were coming back from the cemetery,' Rifke said, saying the words in slow Afrikaans. 'Then we met Izula –'

Mevrou van Niel darted a look at Willem.

'And he – he disappeared,' Rifke finished.

Piet said something. Rifke caught only the words 'Anton and Izula'. Hendrik laughed and was about to whisper something back when Mevrou smacked the table with the flat of her hand.

'Enough!' she said, and the boys were immediately silenced. They bowed their heads, but Rifke could see them flicking glances at each other from under their fringes.

Mevrou van Niel pulled the stack of plates towards her and set about dishing out the lunch. Her mouth was a stiff stripe. The bashing of the silver serving spoon against the side of the pot was the only sound in the room. Willem fidgeted in his seat, then stood up.

'I'll go and find him, Moeder,' he said.

'Find who?' Anton said, striding into the room. He dragged his chair out from the table and sat down. He sniffed the air. 'Pork stew. *Lekker!* It is my favourite,' he said, throwing his napkin on to his lap. He looked around. 'What? Why is everybody staring at me?'

'Why are you late to the table?' Mevrou van Niel asked, her green eyes fixed on Anton. 'Pa is not here but the rules is the same.'

Anton said nothing. He pushed his hair away from his forehead.

'Where have you been?' Mevrou persisted. Her left forefinger tapped the table.

'Oh, I just went to close the gates. I did not want the goats to eat your vegetables, Moeder.'

Mevrou van Niel continued to look at him as though she were waiting for something else. Ma sometimes did that to Rifke when she'd given her an explanation and it wasn't the one Ma'd been hoping for. Anton shrugged.

'*Jammer,*' he apologized.

Mevrou closed her eyes and took a deep breath. She opened her eyes and carried on serving the food. Vegetables only for Rifke. Luckily she still had some polony left.

The bathroom was a small room next door to the kitchen, and it was just that – a room with a bath in it. It was an old cast-iron tub with claw-and-ball-feet, strangely fancy for Driemieliesfontein, and Rifke wondered if Cecily Wainwright had insisted on it before agreeing to teach out here in the *bundu*. That evening Mevrou van Niel helped Rifke fill the bath, carrying bowls of hot and cold water from the kitchen. She lit the candle already waiting on the windowsill.

Rifke closed the door behind Mevrou's fading footsteps. She felt for a key in the lock. There wasn't one. Just a huge old-fashioned keyhole through which Rifke could see the passage. Undoing the zip at the back of her dress, she stopped suddenly. No one would come in, or look through the keyhole, would they? But then again, she hadn't thought anyone would come into her room while she was sleeping. She wasn't going to leave it to chance. She opened the bathroom door and ran to her room. The remains of the polony were still wrapped in a tattered piece of brown paper. She snatched up the paper and the chair next to her bed. A few minutes later, she'd wedged the bathroom door shut by jamming the chair under the handle – she'd seen it done in films – and crammed the polony paper into the keyhole. The garlic and pepper smell coming off the wrapper filled the bathroom. It was like having Kalman's butchery right there with her in Driemieliesfontein.

Rifke's face felt tight. The midday sun must have burned her skin. The water scorched the bridge of her nose and her cheeks when she submerged herself. But what a delight it was to soak head to toe in soapy water and, at long last, to wash the dirt and dust and sweat out of her hair.

Scrubbing herself with a still-hard tablet of Sunlight, Rifke felt an ache and a stinging in her upper arm. By the candlelight she made out five purple ovals and five deep half moons, one of them bloody. Izula had left her mark.

Rifke thought about what had happened. Why had Izula been so angry? What could Anton have done to make her so wild? Disappointment nagged at Rifke too. Disappointment that Anton hadn't stayed to protect her. But he was right to think about the goats eating the vegetables Mevrou van Niel tended so carefully. Goats would eat anything and everything. Even Rifke knew that. She touched her arm gingerly. The same question kept returning – what did Izula have against her? She remembered what Anton had said about spells, and her skin contracted into thousands of goose pimples. She shivered despite the heat of the bath water.

Chapter Twenty-Six

Mevrou's continuing reluctance – no, more than that, – refusal – to allow Rifke to help in the house was puzzling.

It wasn't as if she were worried Rifke would dekosher her kitchen – like Ruthie's mother, who hovered around behind anyone who dared to step into her kitchen, fluttering her tiny hands, just in case they set something down on the wrong surface. Of course Ma was worried about that too. Not that there was even the remotest chance of Rifke doing so after nearly fifteen years of loud reminders, and they rarely had anyone else venture further into their flat than the doorway.

And there was never a possibility of Rifke *offering* to help Ma. Nothing in the way Ma ran their flat allowed for anything so genteel, so light of touch. No. Rifke was ordered to do things. Commanded, more accurately. Compared with what she had to put up with, she sometimes thought Pharaoh's slaves had had nothing to complain about.

And now Rifke was almost begging to be given something to do. Was it pride that made Mevrou van Niel shake her head when Rifke offered to knead the bread or polish the peach-pip kitchen floor? She felt ill at ease just sitting about doing nothing. And it made each day feel long and empty.

Mevrou cleared up after breakfast, then she and the boys set forth to carry out their jobs on the farm. They left Rifke standing in the middle of the kitchen, listening to the clatter of their boots fading to silence. She paced the room, her hands dug deeply into the pockets of the trousers she was wearing again. She could hear the lowing of the cows. Piet or Hendrik calling out. Mevrou answering.

'I've had enough!' Rifke said out loud, slapping her hand against the tabletop.

She strode down the passage and out through the back garden. She pushed open gates and slammed them shut behind her. Past the cowsheds she marched, past the barns and the pigpens and the chicken coop, and past the tractor left to rust in a corner of a field. Mevrou van Niel was in the stretch of land designated as her vegetable field. Rifke could barely make her out, kneeling in the furrows: she was dressed in shades of brown, a dun-coloured man's hat on her head. Camouflaged. She was digging up potatoes, dusting the soil off them and placing them in a hessian sack she'd hung across her body and over her back.

Rifke stumbled, unused to walking across the crusty ribs of soil. Mevrou van Niel raised her head. She shielded her eyes against the sun.

'Rebecca?' Perhaps there was something in the way

Rifke was looking at her, or the fact that she was panting. Mevrou's eyes widened and she staggered to her feet. 'Something is happened to my sons?'

Rifke put up her hand. 'No, no. I'm sorry. I'm sorry I gave you a fright.' She paused for a moment. 'Mevrou van Niel. I've come to help.' She waved at the expanse of browns and ochre around them. 'Please don't stop me. I can pick vegetables or fruit . . . anything. I have to help.'

Mevrou put one hand to her back. The thumb of her other hand worked at the soil under her fingernails. She said nothing for a moment. Just looked into the distance. A trickle of sweat met the collar of her shirt. Rifke shifted her weight. Some earth crumbled beneath her boots. Mevrou turned back to Rifke. She wiped at the sweat, leaving a smear. She nodded once and got down on to her knees again, passing an empty sack to Rifke.

They were out in the field for a few hours. Mevrou didn't speak and Rifke didn't want to disturb her. Rifke felt the sun beating at the back of her neck and across her face. Her back was hurting too, the muscles burning. Mevrou stopped to look at the sky. She got slowly to her feet, easing her bones into position. Taking off her hat, she wiped her forehead with her sleeve.

'Come, Rebecca. It is now time to stop. These *artappels* . . . potatoes . . . we have digged, we must shall put these in the . . .'

She felt for the word, then after a moment abandoned

the search. Between them they had filled six sacks. There was a large wheelbarrow at the end of the field. Mevrou brought it over to where Rifke was standing. They'd just loaded it with three of the sacks when Willem appeared. He was carrying a reel of wire and his toolbox.

'Rebecca –' He glanced at his mother, apparently surprised to see Rifke there. He'd seen Mevrou refuse Rifke's many offers of help. Rifke felt a small thrill of victory.

Mevrou van Niel ignored his questioning look. She pointed at the wire.

'Do you think you will be able to mend the fence, Willem?'

'*Ja*, Moeder. I was up there earlier.' Rifke was finding it easier to understand the Afrikaans they spoke. 'I can see where the jackal got in,' he continued. 'The trouble is, jackals – they is so cunning. It will find another way in before long. I have told Anton to keep the sheep away from the land up there.'

It was the longest speech Rifke had ever heard him make.

'I will take these potatoes to the storeroom.' He set his stuff down on the ground, loaded the other bags of potatoes and bent to lift the handles of the wheelbarrow. Mevrou pressed her hands into the small of her back for a moment or two. She and Rifke followed him as he made his knock-kneed way back towards the farm buildings, pushing the wheelbarrow.

The storeroom was in the cellar of the dairy, itself a small outbuilding not far away from the cowsheds. Stepping inside was like stepping into smooth, cold water, instantly soothing to Rifke's hot face. The sour milk smell of the dairy gave way to the sweet smell of apples as they climbed down the ladder into the cellar. Willem left as soon as he'd carried the sacks of potatoes down after them.

The walls were lined with wooden racks, a few of which held apples.

'From last year,' Mevrou explained. She showed Rifke an apple whose skin was just beginning to pucker like an old lady's upper lip. She put it back in the rack. 'I have seen some of the orange trees is having ripe oranges. Tomorrow we must start to pick them.'

Rifke stared at her back. Had she really said 'we'?

Together they poured the potatoes into the empty racks. There was something satisfying in the drumming of the potatoes as they hit the wood, knocking the smell of the earth off each other. Rifke folded the empty sacks. Mevrou stashed them in the corner. They made their way back towards the house and into the kitchen, where they scrubbed their hands in silence – a silence Rifke now felt was companionable. She felt more comfortable now that she'd helped out in the field, as though she'd begun to earn her keep. Later she didn't mind so much when Mevrou refused to let her help with the lunch.

Chapter Twenty-Seven

Mevrou van Niel ran her finger over the bottles on the top shelf of the kitchen cupboard.

'I is sorry, Rebecca. Nothing. I has nothing for you.' She shook her head. 'It is my fault this has happened.'

All the time that Rifke had been out in the field the day before, the sun had continued the work it had begun on Sunday, blowtorching her forehead, nose and cheeks and the back of her neck until the skin bubbled. It hurt to blink, hurt to smile.

At Muizenberg beach two years before, Aunty had urged Ma to get into a bathing suit and the sun had reached in under the beach umbrella and grilled Ma's shoulders. Ma had given Rifke some stuff to paint on to her skin. What had it been? Rifke remembered Ma sitting in the bedroom of the boarding house, imprisoned in her corset, cursing Aunty, the stuff cracking like dried glue over her skin. Outside, the shriek of seagulls and the roar of the sea. It was funny how her memories felt unreal – more like imagined scenes than things that had really happened. Rifke touched her face with the tips of her fingers.

'You must better not go outside, Rebecca.' Mevrou

van Niel closed the cupboard and unhooked her basket from its nail.

'But I wanted – I was going to help pick the oranges,' Rifke said. Tears pricked her eyes. She blinked them away. How on earth was she going to spend another day inside doing nothing? Especially after Mevrou had given in and allowed her to help with the potatoes.

Mevrou put up her hand. 'Piet and Hendrik, they will help.' She moved towards the door. 'Anton and Willem too.'

Rifke listened to the scuff and clump of her boots going down the passage, and the click of the door to the back garden as she shut it behind her. She took a cup off the draining board and pumped some water into it. She sat down at the table.

From somewhere outside Sibu gave a piercing scream, followed by another. Rifke sat up. Should she go and see? Izula was out there too; Rifke heard her admonish him. No. She should definitely not go out. As Izula's behaviour on Sunday had shown, Izula didn't want Rifke to have anything to do with Sibu. His cries faded. Izula must be taking him away. Rifke lifted the cup to her face and pressed it gently against her skin.

'Has you seen my mother?' Anton appeared, his bare feet as silent as usual. He peered at her. 'Hell, your face is red!' He grinned and put out his hands. 'I can warm myself on you!' He put two fingers against her cheek and made a hissing sound. 'Sizzling hot!'

Rifke smiled and ducked her head.

'Anton!' Willem said. He'd appeared in the doorway. 'Moeder says bring the ladders. For the oranges. Now. She needs them now.'

'*Ja, ja*. Keep yourself calm, *boetie*. I is coming.' He stood up straight and stretched his arms high above his head. His shirt lifted. Rifke could see the muscled ridges of his stomach. 'Anyway – what's the matter with you, little Willem? Why you not carrying them yourself? Too weak, hey?'

Willem's face darkened. He scowled at Anton. 'Just do what Moeder asks,' he said.

Anton winked at Rifke, then turned to leave the room, knocking into Willem as he went out. 'Oops. Sorry. I is very clumsy.'

Playfighting? Was that how brothers were? Rifke wondered. Sisters too? She'd never really spent enough time with Mirele to find out.

Willem went into the laundry. He came out carrying a stack of shallow wooden trays – the kind used to store and carry fruit. One tipped off the top and skidded across the floor to Rifke's feet. She bent to pick it up. When she stood to balance it on top of the pile, his eyes opened wide and he took a sharp breath.

'Rebecca – your face. That is very painful.'

'I'm not used to the sun.'

'*Ja*, the sun, it is very strong. On Sunday I was worried. Yesterday also.' His face flushed as he spoke to her.

He was back to his normal awkward self. 'Has my mother gived . . . given you some medicine?'

Rifke shook her head. 'No. She hasn't got any. But it – it's all right.' His awkwardness was making her embarrassed. She began to gabble. 'I'll be all right if I just stay inside for a while. It's a shame – I've never had a chance to pick oranges before, you know, off a tree.'

Willem nodded. He stood for a second longer, not saying anything, his eyes sliding away from hers. Rifke looked away too. A fly vibrated against the window. Willem gave the trays a shake to settle them better in his arms, then clattered out of the kitchen.

Rifke slumped over the table, holding her head carefully in her hands. Even her scalp felt tender. She needed to remember what that liquid had been. Not milk. Not butter. The mixture had been white and frothy. Egg white! Ma must have whisked it a bit before Rifke applied it.

The basket in which Mevrou van Niel kept eggs was empty. Rifke hadn't yet been to the chicken coop, but she knew where it was. She made for the door to the back garden. As she opened it, the sun jabbed her face with a million sharp needles. She stepped back inside and shut the door. Perhaps Mevrou would bring some eggs in with her when she'd finished picking oranges.

Rifke went to her bedroom and shut the door behind

her. Once again, there was nothing for her to do – and it was tiring. She opened the little window near her bed, hoping for a breeze, and lay down on her bed, setting her head on the pillow as carefully as she could.

By the time she opened her eyes again, an hour or two must have passed. Her throat parched, she decided to fetch herself a glass of water. Swinging her legs off the bed, she staggered towards the door. As she drew it shut behind her, her hand closed on something rustly. Some-one had hung a broad-brimmed straw hat on her door handle. She lifted it off and saw a name stitched in spindly backstitch round the inside lining.

'Cecily Wainwright,' Rifke read out loud. She glanced up and down the empty passage. Whoever had left the hat on her door wasn't around any longer, but she was sure she knew who it had been.

'Anton.' Tenderness crept through her like warm honey, and she smiled.

She stroked the faded fabric daisies around the brim. After he'd left her to fend off Izula she'd begun to wonder if she'd imagined all his glances in her direction, his touching her arm and shoulder, his acts of kindness. The hat was a clear sign that she hadn't. He made her feel cared for, out here in the *bundu*. He was looking out for her. She put the hat on. It was slightly big, but that was fine because her skin and scalp were so tender. She tied the ribbons under her chin before leaving the house. Now she could get the eggs herself.

The chickens had a large fenced-off area as their run, far larger than Mrs Kossoff's back garden. The stench, though, hit Rifke's nostrils and the back of her throat in just the same way.

'I wonder which one of these Ma would eat,' Rifke murmured wistfully, looking at the hens through the fence. Definitely not the tattered ones, nor the stringy ones with evil eyes.

She pushed open the door to the shed. Its creak sent a clutch of hens off in a shudder of panic. Rifke shrieked, and then felt ashamed of herself. Glad too that there was no one around to hear her. She held back, waiting until the squawking and fluttering had died down, then took a few tentative steps further into the shed. It was dark. And it stank.

'Bring back the Egg Man,' she said into the darkness. Every Wednesday he knocked on the door to their flat in his grubby overcoat, his huge basket of eggs over one arm. Week after week he unfurled the scrap of grey blanket that covered them with the same look of surprise and delight. And week after week Ma sent him on his way. They'd tried his eggs twice, and every one of them had been off. Dinosaurs' eggs, Ma said.

But at least they hadn't had to do this. Rifke picked her way across the floor, which she could tell even through the thick soles of her boots was crunchy and slippery with old and fresh chicken kak. Going to Mrs Kossoff was revolting, but this was worse. Rifke posed her thumb and forefinger into a pincer shape, ready to lower into a nest and grab an egg. She approached one of the dark shapes sitting on the nests.

A vicious mother hen, she discovered, rubbing her hand. How was she going to get hold of the eggs?

The door creaked. Rifke looked round.

'Sibu!' she called out.

He was sniffing a little. Ignoring Rifke, he made straight for the nests, shoved the hens aside, grabbed the eggs and put them in the bowl he was carrying. Speed was clearly the secret. Rifke copied him, and her reward was three eggs. Still warm – she could feel them through the cotton of her shirt.

She followed him out. An egg fell out of his bowl. It rolled on to the soil and he bent to pick it up, still sniffing.

'Sibu, wait.' Rifke looked around to see if Izula was anywhere before putting her hand on his shoulder.

He looked up at her.

'What's wrong, Sibu?' Rifke knelt to look at him. She gasped. 'Oh my goodness! Your ears!' Instead of reeds, there was now a piece of twig in each of his earlobes. Quite thick twigs. And around each twig the skin of his earlobes was puffy and clotted with blood. And smeared with some stuff that looked like congealed animal fat. Rifke felt a surge of anger. How could Izula hurt her own child like that?

Sibu looked at Rifke, his eyes glassy with unfallen

tears. She felt in her trouser pocket for something to clean his ears with.

A raucous cry tore the air. Both Rifke and Sibu started. The sound seemed to hang there like a rag caught in a gust of wind. Then it fell away.

Izula was standing about twenty paces from them, a kid under her arm. She dropped it. It lay where it landed, trembling a little. A black cross, a shadow on the ground, caught Rifke's attention. Izula was looking at it too. Then she stared at Rifke before slowly tilting her face towards the sky. Immediately her eyes widened, and her face tightened into a look of dreadful fear.

'Sibu!' she screamed, and ran towards him, her arms stretched out in front of her.

Rifke looked up. A dark bird was hovering directly above them. Near enough for Rifke to make out its hammer-shaped head and sharp beak. It moved, and the cross-shadow its wings made settled first on Rifke, and then on Sibu.

Izula swept her son into her arms, pressing his head against her body, one of her hands splayed over the back of his head. She was panting as she backed away, casting terrified glances from Rifke to the bird and back to Rifke.

The bird hovered for a second or two before emitting a screech and gliding off.

'*Tekwane!*' Izula shouted.

Rifke didn't know what that meant, and didn't know

why Izula seemed to link her with the bird. It made her feel uneasy. She would tell Anton about it. He'd said all that spells stuff was nonsense. She needed him to reassure her again.

Chapter Twenty-Eight

The heat had been building. The air shimmered with it. It made everything look molten and bendy. The handle of the lavatory door burned your hand if you touched it without a cloth, and the inside of the shack was an oven.

A hot wind came off the mountains and blew the dry soil around, through keyholes and gaps in the window frames and the holes in the roof, until everything was covered with ochre powder. Sweat mingled with it to make a paste, and it was hard to breathe. There was a permanent coating of grit at the back of Rifke's throat. Putting one foot in front of the other was an effort. Even Mevrou opened the top button of her shirt and rolled her sleeves above her elbows.

In the evening darkness fell suddenly, like the curtain dropped quickly at the end of a play. It brought a little relief from the heat – but not from the mosquitoes, which kept them indoors. Mevrou sat in front of her plate of food. She pushed the roast chicken around before abandoning it altogether. It was unlike her. Even Rifke knew that.

'What is wrong, Moeder?' Willem asked.

Piet and Hendrik were looking at their mother too. Anton was not at the table. He'd been away for a few days at the furthest boundary of Driemieliesfontein, keeping a lookout for the jackal that had found its way in again and killed three more sheep. With every mealtime that he wasn't there, Rifke's yearning to see him grew. She wanted to thank him for the hat, and she needed to talk to him about the bird, and Izula. Besides which, she missed him.

Mevrou van Niel pulled her collar away from the back of her neck. A few strands of her fine hair fell out of her bun. She wove them back into place.

'Moeder?' Willem prompted.

'It is . . . It is just the heat.' She sounded tired. Rifke knew enough about Mevrou to know that she didn't usually show anyone her worries, at least not the younger boys. But Rifke had seen her looking at the almost-empty reservoir earlier that day, and heard her sighing. They needed water.

'Don't worry, Moeder,' Piet said. 'It's going to rain. Then everything will be all right. You'll see. I spotted a hammerhead the other day. It was flying over Driemieliesfontein. She . . .' He pointed at Rifke. 'She saw it too.'

Rifke flushed to think she'd been observed without her knowing. Had he also witnessed Izula's strange behaviour?

'Izula thinks there will be a storm if a hammerhead flies over. Anton told me,' Piet said.

'And she thinks someone will get killed,' Hendrik added.

Rifke's blood chilled. So that was why Izula had grabbed Sibu like that. More omens and magic. But what did that have to do with Rifke?

Meanwhile, Hendrik had turned to Mevrou van Niel. 'That's just rubbish, isn't it, Moeder? Anton says Izula is a witch, but Christians don't believe in that nonsense, do we?'

Mevrou van Niel wiped her forehead. She shook her head. She looked absent. Perhaps she was thinking about Meneer van Niel, fighting far away in Italy. Willem glanced at her. He looked concerned.

'Piet, Hendrik. It's late,' he said. 'Time for bed.'

'No, it's not!'

'We're not going to bed now.' Piet and Hendrik drew together, united.

Willem took no notice of their protests. He pushed his glasses back into place and herded the boys out of the room.

Mevrou took a handkerchief out of her apron pocket and wiped the back of her neck. Then she bowed her head, lacing her hands over the hanky. Rifke collected the dinner things together. Quietly, so as not to disturb Mevrou.

A storm. A death. Rifke stood in front of the sink. Goose pimples sprung up over her skin. She wrapped her arms around herself. How could just seeing a bird mean that would happen? So primitive, she thought, and shook her head, trying to shrug off the bad feeling. Jewish people would never believe that. She reached for a jug of water to pour over the dirty plates.

But a memory stabbed her mind. She stopped, her hand grasping the handle of the jug: Ma spitting. *Tfu! Tfu! Tfu!* Three times she would spit. To ward off the evil eye. What was that, if not primitive? Rifke turned back to the sink. And that was just one of Ma's superstitions. Superstition, religion. Religion . . . superstition. Where did one end and the other begin?

Rifke had always hated Ma's peculiarness. It made Rifke impatient. And embarrassed. She watched the water sluicing over the plates. Ma had told her how her husband had been chosen for her, how she'd arrived with a stranger in a strange new country. The heat, the bustle of Johannesburg, the cars, the trams, surrounded by people she didn't understand and couldn't talk to, thousands of miles away from her village in Lithuania, her parents, the family's cow, her own narrow bed with the embroidered coverlet. Rifke rubbed her eyes. Perhaps she'd been too impatient with Ma. Too quick to feel shame.

Chapter Twenty-Nine

'Shoo! It's still hot out there!'

Rifke swung round. She couldn't stop herself from smiling.

'You're back!' she said. She put down the plate she'd been washing and dried her hands on her trousers. Her hair was hanging down in sweaty strips and she quickly wiped it away from her face.

Anton moved across the kitchen, but somehow without his usual grace. There was something uncoordinated in the way he dodged a chair not yet pushed in under the table. Perhaps Mevrou noticed it too. She'd lifted her head from her prayers slowly, then jerked upright and got to her feet.

'Where have you been?' Her voice was clipped and dry. She drummed two fingers on the edge of the table.

'You know, Moeder.' He laughed. 'Up there by the north fence. Looking for jackals.' He growled and snarled, imitating a wild animal, and laughed again, catching Rifke's eye.

Rifke smiled. But she'd noticed Mevrou flinch, and it made her feel a little uncertain. She'd never seen Mevrou like that – angry, hostile even. And afraid.

Mevrou narrowed her eyes. 'I asked you to be back in

time for dinner today. You said you would. That is why I am asking you where you have been.' She jerked her chin at his head. 'You didn't come straight back, did you? Why is your hair wet?'

For the first time Rifke noticed Anton's hair. His shirt was partially unbuttoned; his neck, the bead necklace and the top of his chest were wet too. Just as on her first morning at Driemieliesfontein. Anton shook his head like a dog, sprinkling water droplets that sparkled briefly in the candlelight.

'*Ag*, I just threw a bucket of water over me.' He turned his back on his mother. 'I need a drink.'

Anton moved towards the sink. He brushed against Rifke as he leaned to take a cup from the stack she'd washed. A strange mixture of smells lingered in the air around him: something burnt and a bit acrid, and that same smell that Rifke'd noticed on Izula's breath – yeasty, and again, for some reason, naggingly familiar.

He pumped up a cupful of water and swallowed it in a gulp. He leaned across Rifke to put the cup in the sink, looking into her face as he did so. There was something loose in his face, a slackness. He didn't seem quite focused. He smiled at her again, but it didn't relate to the brooding look in his eyes. She frowned with concern. Perhaps he'd caught some sort of chill, camping out all night.

'Anton.' Mevrou's voice was unnaturally loud. 'Anton,' she repeated.

'*Ja*, Moeder.' He turned slowly to look at his mother. 'What is it?'

'You know . . .' Mevrou van Niel glanced at Rifke, then sealed her mouth. She shook her head. 'You better eat something.' Stiff-backed, she reached for the roasting dish in which Anton's share of the chicken still lay waiting. She scooped it out on to a plate. It made a scraping noise as she pushed it across the table. What was Mevrou not saying?

Rifke left the room as quietly as her heavy boots would allow. She took a lantern with her. She would need it when she went out to the outhouse later.

Mevrou had sewn Rifke a couple of nightdresses out of some old sheets. After a quick wash using water she'd carried through to her room earlier, Rifke took off the heavy trousers and shirt that had become her uniform. She pulled one of the nighties over her head and arms, enjoying its billow before it floated down around her legs. After that first embarrassing time in Mevrou's enormous nightdress, Rifke didn't want to be seen again in her nightwear by any of the Van Niels. But it was such a hot night, and she yearned for the lightness of the cotton against her skin. She grabbed her cardigan before she left the room, just in case she should run into any of the boys on the way to or from the lavatory.

From down the passage she could hear Mevrou's voice, and Anton's raised in reply. She couldn't hear what they were saying. Half tempted to listen, she paused a moment, but when she heard Willem saying something to the younger boys from the doorway to their bedroom, she snatched up the lantern and made a dash for the side door. She caught a glimpse of Anton leaving the kitchen, and she wondered again if he were unwell.

Outside, the air was hot and still. Not a calm stillness though. More like an exhausted silence, a burnt-out sort of quiet. But it was lovely to be wearing the loose night-dress and to feel it swirl around her. Its soft swish around her ankles and the crunch of her boots on the parched soil, interrupted now and then by Leeu's baying in the distance, were the only sounds.

'Goodness! It's still hot,' Rifke murmured as she turned the lavatory door handle. It was still boiling inside too. Rifke held her nose as usual as she locked the door behind her. She smiled at Judy Garland's eyes looking over the tractor advertisement now glued over her. Rifke had just finished when she heard a scuffing noise coming from the other side of the door.

'I'll be out in a minute,' she called. She put on her cardigan and unlocked the door.

'Oh, hello.'

The flat of his hand smashed her in the centre of her chest, pushing her backwards. Backwards. Into the shack. Knocked. The air. Out of her. She seized for breath. His was hot on her neck. Hot and fast. His chest heaving against hers. Shoving her. Back, back, back. Against the seat. Pinioning her to its edge with his knee. One hand against her mouth. Pressing down. Acrid smell. Other hand clawing at the hem of her nightie. Dragging, scraping it upwards, nails in her skin, breathing heavily all the while, panting in her ear. Her arms useless, battering his back, hammering, trying to keep her nightdress down, kicking. Screaming into the sweaty palm. His belt buckle biting into her, hand all the time pulling at her nightie, tearing. Judy Garland's laughing eyes. His eyes. Wild.

She bit into his palm. He jerked his hand away and her scream burst into the air.

'Stop! Help! Help me! Someone help me!'

Sobs broke in her throat. She spat in his face just before his hand clamped her face again. His eyes fixed on hers. He stopped pulling at her nightdress for a second. Thank goodness thank goodness thank goodness.

And then with a growl of impatience, his nails raking at her chest, he grabbed the neckline of her nightie.

Chapter Thirty

Tiny red and white beads peppered Rifke. Like thousands of sharp bullets, they stung her neck and face.

'You animal!' Willem shouted.

He had one hand in the band of what remained of Anton's necklace. There was enough of it left to make Anton choke. His face bulged, dark red. He was gurgling and spluttering. More beads shot off. Rifke heard their tinny ping as they bounced around the shack.

'Let go of her, you disgusting . . .' Willem grabbed Anton's long hair and yanked it backwards. 'Didn't you hear what I said? Let go. Now!'

Rifke felt Anton loosen his grip on her nightdress. She sank backwards. The floor was hot. But she was freezing cold. She wanted to curl into the corner, but her body wouldn't move. Her eyes were wide open. She wanted to shut them, but they wouldn't close.

Willem dragged Anton out of the shack. Anton pulled away, but Willem's hands were firmly wound into his collar and his hair. Anton tried to shout something. His voice came out strangled and high pitched. Rifke heard their footsteps on the dry earth outside. There was a scuffle. Swearing. The thwack of a fist making contact with flesh. More scuffling. Silence. Then footsteps coming back towards the shack. Rifke froze. Oh, please no.

'Are you all right, Rebecca?' Willem crouched next to her. '*Ag*, stupid of me to ask that. Of course you is not.' He put his hand out, but he didn't touch her. 'He is gone, Rebecca.'

She was shaking so much that it looked to her like Willem was vibrating. There was blood running down the side of his face. She stared at the pattern it was making as it dripped on to his shirt. 'W-what?' she said.

'Anton. He is gone now. He will not . . . bother you again. I will make sure of that.' He had his glasses in his hand. They were twisted. Bending them this way and that, he reworked the wire frames and wound them back on to his face. 'When you is – are – ready I will go with you back into the house. But only when you want to.' He sat down just outside the doorway.

After a few minutes Rifke staggered to her feet, dragging her cardigan closed around her. The tremble in her legs made her hold on to the wall to steady herself. Quickly Willem stood too. Thank goodness he didn't try to touch her. But for the first time ever she was glad he was there. He looked at her just like he'd looked at his mother earlier – eyes clouded with concern.

He picked up the lantern. Together they walked slowly back to the house, Rifke hunched over and shivering. He kept just the right amount of space between them.

As they reached the door, Rifke turned to him.

'Thank you,' she whispered. Tears welled in her eyes. 'I-I don't know what – I mean – if you hadn't turned up when you did –'

Willem frowned. 'It is my fault.' He fisted his hands. 'I know what . . . Anton –' he spat his brother's name out – 'is like. I am sorry. Please, Rebecca, forgive me. I should have watched over you better.'

'No, no. That is not right,' Rifke tried to say, but her throat had thickened with pent-up sobs.

The door swung open. Mevrou van Niel's face looked ghostly in the glow of her candle.

'What goes here on?' she said in English, looking from Rifke to Willem. Her eye fell on Willem's cut face. Gasping, she leaped forward, one hand reaching for his head. 'Who has done this?' She darted a look at Rifke.

'No, Moeder.' Willem held his hand up to fend off hers. 'It was Anton.' He looked at Rifke and gestured at her torn nightdress. 'Anton – he tried to –'

Rifke looked up at Mevrou van Niel. Through the blur of her tears she could see a look of horror flit across Mevrou's white face. And then almost as quickly, her closed-off expression was back again. Mevrou blinked twice. Her hand fluttered in mid-air, then dropped against her side. She spun on her heel, her boot squeaking on the wooden floor. Rifke heard her going into her bedroom and the click of the door as she shut it behind her.

Rifke wiped her eyes, not sure if she'd seen correctly. 'Rebecca . . .' Willem was lost for words.

How could she? How could she look at Rifke's face and the scratches on her chest and the tears in her night-dress – and do nothing? Ma wouldn't have done that. Ma . . . Sobs tore through Rifke's chest. She couldn't breathe. The passage began to spin around her, Willem's frowning face whirling with it. Rifke pushed past him and ran to her room. She shut the door and slid to the floor, burying her head in her hands.

She wanted Ma. She wanted Ma's fat arms around her, and Ma's smell of Omo washing powder and fried fish and fresh bread and face cream. She wanted Ma's hands patting her softly on the back and the Yiddish words she murmured into Rifke's hair. Rifke cried into the cardigan Ma had knitted for her, pulling it up around her head, trying to breathe deeply enough into the stitches to find the smell of Ma again.

Chapter Thirty-One

Rifke lay on the floor worn out from crying. Slowly she became aware of feeling cold. The floor was hard. Her limbs ached as though she'd walked a thousand miles. Her face felt bruised and the scratches up her legs and on her chest rang with pain. She pushed herself into a sitting position.

'Must . . . get . . . into bed,' she muttered. Using the door as a support, she got to her feet. Froze. What if he came back? What if he came into her room while she was asleep? She remembered that night when there'd been someone in her room. Not for one second had she suspected Anton. Bile rose in her throat and she began to shake again. She fumbled for the lock beneath the door handle. There was no key. Never had been. How could she secure the door?

She looked around the room. In the grainy darkness she could make out the chair next to her bed. Moving like an old lady, she shuffled over to get it and wedged it under the door handle. With fingers made clumsy by panic, she checked it. It was firmly in place. But he was strong. He could knock that chair into a spray of splinters. Rifke could almost see it happening, hear the crack of the hundred-year-old wood, its dry burst, followed by the light scuff of his bare feet moving across the floor. She stood in the dark, trembling. Helpless.

'Rebecca, it is Willem. You must not be afraid.' She heard the whispered words through the keyhole. 'He will not come near to you. I will make sure of that. I am here on the other side of your door. All the night I will stay.'

The blue canvas bag was lying on the floor. Rifke picked it up before making her way to the bed, and climbing in. She bundled herself under the covers. She cradled the bag. The garlic ghost of the polony was still strong enough to be comforting.

The night crept past. Rifke watched its shadow crawling across the walls. The room still held the day's heat, but Rifke didn't know whether she felt cold or hot, the memory of Anton making her shiver one minute and sweat the next. As the room lightened, a growl of thunder broke the silence. The trees outside began to rattle their bones, and a gust of wind hissed through the window above Rifke's head.

The hammerhead bird. A storm. A death. Rifke stiffened.

One rumble followed another, an imprecation, the final notes of the curse fading almost to nothing, before rising to a deafening roar. Rifke started each time and clutched the blue bag closer to her. Back in Johannesburg, she'd always loved the late-afternoon storms. They were like a violent argument, followed by tears. Over quickly. But that was a hundred years ago, when she'd watched the leaden sky and the rain from the window in their flat, Ma in the background, clattering about, making supper.

Lightning sparked. Her room jumped, blue-white. Rifke sat up, gathering the bedclothes round her neck. Was the hammerhead responsible for the storm? Could Izula have called it up somehow? Rifke shuddered.

With a swoosh, rain began to fall. The drips through the holes in the roof started slowly, some hitting Rifke's bed, some landing on the floor. Mesmerized, she watched them in the juddering light as they gathered speed and volume. When the bed-linen was too sodden to ignore, she got out of bed and pushed it out of the range of the water. The potty that had been under the bed made a useful vessel. She positioned it under the biggest hole. Still – it wasn't going to be long before it was full. Where could she empty it? It was miles too big to fit through the window. Did she dare open the door? She paced the room, her arms crossed in front of her stomach.

'Rebecca – the rain – it is coming in, yes?' Willem asked from the other side of the door.

Rifke moved to the door. She put her ear against it.

'Rebecca? I has – have – here a bowl to catch the water.'

She removed the chair from under the handle and opened the door a fraction.

In the half-light, Willem looked a sorry sight. Blood from his cut was smeared across his face; his hair was, as usual, tangled in his glasses, and it too was bloodied. He nudged the crooked frame closer to his eyes, and Rifke noticed that his knuckles were bruised. He bent down to lift a huge copper bowl from the floor.

'Grandma Cecily slept in this room. Always the rain was coming through the roof,' he said. 'Pa said he would fix it.' He frowned. 'I must fix it,' he muttered. 'Well, here is the bowl. It is I think big enough for the two holes in the roof.'

'Thank you,' Rifke said, opening the door wider to take it from him. She wondered which of them looked worse. 'And – thank you also – you know, for sitting out here.'

He ducked his head and made a vague gesture with his hand. 'I is here still if you needs – need – me.'

He shut the door behind her. Rifke heard the creak of the wood as he rested his back against it.

She set the bowl on the floor and sat on the bed, listening to the ring of the drops against the copper change to splashes as the bowl filled.

Fifteen days until the train. She knew without having to check the calendar. She'd been wearing Cecily Wainwright's hat. Now it turned out she'd been sleeping in her bed. What next? The grave with the rock headstone loomed in her mind.

Tears filled her eyes again. Looking down at her bare feet, she clicked her heels together. Then closed her eyes.

'There's no place like home. There's no place like home. There's no place like home.'

Chapter Thirty-Two

It had been raining for over a week, relenting only long enough for Willem to make makeshift repairs to the thatch. But still it found a way through, and Rifke lay awake every night listening to the steady drip from the roof into the copper bowl. She'd hardly slept since Anton had attacked her, even though Willem had found the key to her bedroom and she'd been locking herself in every night.

And the days were longer than ever: there was nothing for Rifke to do in the house. Mevrou refused to meet her questioning eyes. Why hadn't she warned her about Anton? Rifke had seen her flinch from him, she knew exactly what he was like. And yet Rifke had also seen the long, benevolent gaze that Mevrou sometimes lavished on her eldest son: love, mixed up with her dependence on his strength, and his – Rifke felt for the right word – his manliness, she supposed. At the table, Mevrou's fingers picked at the handles of her cutlery or the edge of the tablecloth, but she barely spoke. She knows, Rifke thought again. She knows he is violent and she can't acknowledge it. Not to herself, and not to me.

In the silence, broken only by the repeated sounds made by the tapping of Mevrou's nails, Piet and Hendrik

sensed something was wrong; they looked at her quizzically whenever Anton's name was mentioned.

Anton himself was up at one of the boundaries of the farm – the river flooded, the fencing washed away, sheep drowned. Perhaps, despite everything Rifke thought of her, Mevrou had banished him there. Or perhaps it was a lucky coincidence. Either way – what a relief it was not to have to see him every day. But Rifke didn't know when he might return, and that made her constantly uneasy. She kept looking over her shoulder, her ears tuned to hear the friction of his feet against the wooden floor.

Going to the outhouse had never been pleasant. Now it filled her with a fear that churned her stomach with acid and pummelled her heart until she could hear it beating in her ears. Willem had swept the lavatory floor, but tiny stray beads from Anton's necklace still grated under the soles of her boots.

She'd chosen a stone from the garden. Large, with flinty points all over it. It filled her hand. She carried it in the pocket of her trousers, taking it out and gripping it in readiness during every visit to the lavatory.

Lying in her bed, Rifke looked at the calendar in the early-morning light. She knew the dates off by heart, but it was so satisfying to scratch out the passing days. It was 29th January. Her birthday. She was fifteen. No handmade card from Ruthie. No parcel from Aunty and Uncle containing books and a tin of Farieda's biscuits. No lopsided cake from Ma. Rifke wiped her eyes and took a deep breath. Eight days to go. Keep going, she murmured. Only eight days.

For the first time in a week, she heard birdsong. The roof had stopped dripping. Watery sunlight from the tiny window cast a square on the floor. Rifke sat up. The rain had stopped. That was a good thing. She needed to get out, get some fresh air and a change of scene. She got up, pulled on her clothes, unlocked the door and made her way outside.

'Sibu!'

He was lying in the grass in the back garden. Rifke ran towards him. Wearing just a vest, he was covered in mud.

'Sibu!' Rifke called his name again, kneeling over him. He stirred, moved one arm a little. Slowly he opened his eyes. They looked lifeless, red-rimmed. He closed them again. His face was covered in a fine sweat and his tight curls were smeared to his head. Yet he was shivering. She felt his forehead. Boiling hot. Rifke stood up. She ran to the garden gate and looked around.

'Izula!' she called. She opened the gate and ran to the outbuilding where Izula lived. 'Izula?' The door was open. Rifke didn't dare go in. She called again. No response. Where was she?

Rifke ran back to the baby. He made a sound and she bent over him. He was breathing quickly. Too quickly. Sibu needed help fast. She swept him into her arms. His body was limp. Rifke saw that the twigs in his earlobes had been replaced with bone discs. They were wider in diameter than the twigs had been. His earlobes had split where the discs had been forced into place. Worse than that, the ears were scabbed with blood and oozing greenish pus.

'Oh, Sibu!' Rifke said, settling him against her chest. 'I will find some medicine for you.' She ran with him into the house. 'I'm not Toiba Lubetkin's daughter for nothing,' she said under her breath.

Rifke carried him into the kitchen. Mevrou kept medicine in one of the cupboards. The room was empty. Everyone else had had breakfast and left, judging by the crockery stacked on the drainer. All the better, Rifke thought. She laid Sibu on the floor, and knelt beside him.

'What would Ma do? Come on, come on, Rifke. Think!' she said out loud. 'A fever. What did she do for a fever? Got to bring down the temperature. Sponge him down.'

Rifke wet a cotton cloth and wiped Sibu's face and body. She kept on doing this until his skin felt cooler. She cleaned the mud off him too. Then she covered his body with a sheet she took from the laundry and rolled up a towel to place under his head. Rummaging through Mevrou's medicines, Rifke found a phial of aspirin, some disinfectant and a bottle of Mercurochrome.

With a bit of trouble she got him to swallow the solution of aspirin she'd made up and a sip or two of water. He fluttered his eyelids but didn't otherwise flinch when she applied disinfectant and Mercurochrome to his ear-lobes, wiping round the horn discs.

She didn't know how long she sat there beside Sibu, sponging him down and feeding him sips of water. Two hours. Three perhaps. Her back was aching and the peach-pip floor was digging into her knees. Mevrou and the boys were probably busy on the farm too far away to return to the house; they would have taken sandwiches with them. Rifke didn't feel like eating. Hadn't for days. She ached for home. For Ma. Especially today. She knew she'd better eat something and was reaching for an apple from the bowl on the table when Willem came flying into the kitchen.

'Oh, phew! There you are, Rebecca,' he said, panting. He took a deep breath. 'I was worried when I knocked on your door, and there wasn't no – an – answer.' He glanced down. 'Sibu! – What has happened to him?'

'I think he has an infection. His ears. They don't look good. He has a temperature.' Rifke stroked Sibu's hair. 'I think it's coming down now. When I found him it was very high.'

Willem knelt next to Rifke. He put the back of his hand against Sibu's forehead, and sighed. 'I will never understand why Anton does not look after his son.'

Rifke stopped mid-stroke. What? Had she heard correctly? And yet, looking at Sibu now, how could she not have recognized Anton's cleft chin and strong jawline?

Willem was still looking at Sibu and hadn't noticed Rifke's shock.

'So are Anton and Izula – married?' Rifke was finding it difficult to grasp the idea of Anton with Izula. And the idea of a black girl with a white boy. She'd never heard of such a thing.

'Not married according to Christians. Not according to Moeder.' He took his glasses off to polish them on his shirt. He looked at Rifke. His eyes were green like Mevrou's, darker than Anton's, one of them still a little puffy where Anton had hit him. The cut to the side of his face had scabbed over. 'But in Izula's beliefs, they is – are – married. That necklace he was wearing – Izula made it for him. It is a sign he belongs to her.'

'But – but –' Rifke was still struggling to understand. 'What about Anton? Doesn't he think he is married?'

'What about him?' Willem scowled. 'He is an animal. Izula arrives here from . . . we doesn't know where. A young girl. Far away from her homeland. Anton follows her. Like a dog, a jackal. He watches, watches. Then one day, he . . .' Willem shot a glance at Rifke, then looked down.

So he'd raped Izula.

Rifke took a deep breath. She thought of Izula, arriving at Driemieliesfontein, hungry and weak and covered in the dry dust of the veld, the two goats her only companions. A young girl, as Willem said – perhaps no more than Rifke's own age. And if she had come from

Zululand, as Mevrou had guessed, then she was hundreds of miles away from her people. Who knew what had brought her so far?

And Rifke thought of Anton offering her the protection she needed, but all the while stalking her, biding his time.

Rifke sighed, and when she stroked his forehead Sibu stirred. He opened his eyes. Giving birth to Sibu must have bound Izula to Anton. It made him hers all the more.

'Sibu?' Rifke bent over him. 'Are you feeling better?' She was glad of the distraction from her disturbing thoughts.

Willem smiled. 'Sibu doesn't understand English, Rebecca.' He translated her question into Afrikaans.

Sibu didn't reply. He held out his arms to be picked up. It was Rifke he wanted. She knelt and lifted him, gathering the sheet around his body. He wound his arms around her neck.

She turned to Willem. 'What should I do? Izula – I don't think she wants me to have anything to do with Sibu. But he needs to be looked after. Should I keep him here? Or should I take him to his house?'

A sound came from the doorway. Izula. How long had she been there? She was wearing a skirt made of goatskin, with a rough blanket around her shoulders. She stood still, the only movement the swaying of her plaits over her face as she breathed heavily.

Rifke found her eyes meeting Izula's, and felt a rush of sympathy for her. They had more in common than Rifke could ever have imagined. Rifke smiled and took a few steps forward, holding Sibu out to her. As before, Izula's eyes were bloodshot, the whites yellowed. She looked wary. As she moved to take Sibu, she stumbled. Rifke rushed to help her, but Izula pushed her aside and grabbed Sibu from her arms. The yeasty smell came off Izula more strongly than ever. It came from her mouth and from her clothes, dense enough to make Rifke feel dizzy.

A memory bubbled to the surface, and suddenly Rifke knew where she'd smelt it before. Late one night, he'd leaned over her, her father, rough hands rattling her cot, and Ma had shoved him away, and he'd shouted, his voice hoarse, and kicked the cot before staggering off. And left behind that same smell radiating now from Izula, a heavy smell that loitered in the air, threatening to smother Rifke. The word she'd overheard Ma use the day they left Kimberley – what was it? *Shikker*. Drunkard. The smell? Alcohol. Beer, probably. Rifke snatched the thought and screwed it up like a piece of paper into a tight ball. It was not something she wanted to examine now.

So Izula had been brewing beer in her room, and – of course – Anton must have been drinking it too.

Sibu stirred as Izula pulled at the sheet covering him. He cried out. Rifke stepped forwards and put her hand on his back.

'Sibu is not well, Izula,' Rifke said in slow Afrikaans. 'I have washed him down. I put . . . um –' she couldn't think of the word for "antiseptic' – 'something on his ears. I gave him also some aspirin. You should give him some more later.'

Izula turned, pulling Sibu away from Rifke, shielding him from her. There was a strange look in her eyes – a mixture of distrust and fear and hurt. For the first time she seemed vulnerable. She held Rifke's gaze for a minute, then Rifke saw her expression harden. Her pupils narrowed to pinpoints and a muscle in her cheek flickered.

She spat out some words and, ripping the sheet off Sibu's body, flung it to the floor. She left the room, lurching slightly. Sibu's head bounced against her shoulder.

Rifke was alarmed. 'Willem – she's – she's been drinking. We can't just let her – what about Sibu? What about his ears? How could she have done such a horrible thing to him?' She leaped forward to go after Izula.

Willem put his hand on her shoulder to stop her. He shook his head. 'Rebecca, it is better we leave her. Izula – she has her own ways. Piercing Sibu's ears – that is just one of them. She believes that it opens the ear of the spirit.'

'But I'm worried about him!'

Willem's smile was gentle. 'It is all right. You have already helped him.'

Chapter Thirty-Three

At the entrance to the family cemetery Willem set down the toolbox he'd been carrying. Rifke stood behind him. The sunlight was bright after the gloom of the kitchen, and it stung her eyes. But what a relief to be out in the open air again. She needed to wipe away the bad feeling her meeting with Izula had left behind.

Willem was busy with the lock to the gate. The clang and tinkle of metal parts sounded loud in the still air. Rifke watched him for a minute, not really taking in what he was doing.

'Why is Izula like that? I was just trying to help Sibu, you know. I would never hurt him.'

Willem turned to look at her. He scratched his head and frowned. 'I think maybe she is worried you will take him away from her. No – not take away, but . . . um, Sibu will like – love – you more than her. Something like that.'

Rifke was shocked. 'But I would never take him away from her. And how could he possibly love me more than her? How can she think that?'

Willem put down the pliers he was holding. He nudged his glasses back into position. 'I suppose it is very *moeilik* – difficult for us to understand. It is to do with being a mother.' He sighed. 'Sibu is all she has.'

He looked down a moment. When he looked up again, he had coloured a little. 'Why is you here? Where is your mother and father, your family?' He put up his hand. 'Sorry, Rebecca – Moeder says it is rude to ask questions.'

Apart from the initial shock at finding her on the farm, it was the first time any of the Van Niels had wanted to know about her. She took a breath. She would have liked to talk about Ma and Mirele, but she couldn't. Not now. Her longing for Ma was too near the surface.

She shook her head. 'I . . . er, will just go to the Malays' cemetery,' she said quickly, pointing to the burial ground she'd noticed that first Sunday.

'*Ja*, OK,' Willem said. He looked uncomfortable. Rifke wanted to reassure him. It was fine to ask questions. More than that – it was lovely that he had.

'Willem – I just – um –'

He'd picked up a hammer and was tapping at a piece of metal. He didn't look up. 'If you needs me, I is here.'

Rifke stood for a second. Then, gathering two handfuls of pebbles from the ground near her feet, she followed the path away from the Van Niel's cemetery.

The area containing the Malays' graves was in a stretch of barren ground. The thorn trees around it made it look even more desolate. Rifke scrabbled through an opening in the fence. She stood still for a moment. There were perhaps thirty or forty graves, some of the markers so old they were little more than stumps of splintered wood. The first Malays must have felt lost in this huge, wide-open land.

'I wonder when people first begin to feel that they belong somewhere,' she said out loud. She swept her gaze over the dry cemetery. 'Perhaps . . . perhaps it's the first time they bury someone.'

The last Malay – when had he or she been buried? And who paid their respects to them? A sadness stole over Rifke. She ran her thumbs over the pebbles she'd collected.

Starting at the far corner, Rifke walked among the graves, stopping at each to set a pebble down. The ones she had over she used to mark out '1944', pushing each pebble into the mud the way Ma pressed glacé cherries into the icing of her birthday cakes. There was a boulder jutting from one corner of the graveyard. Rifke sat down on it.

So many thoughts crowded her mind, jostling to get to the front. Rifke needed to slow them down, to create some order. Izula – of course she would be suspicious of Rifke: Anton, in her eyes, belonged to her. And of course she would be wary of Rifke's attention to Sibu, unhappy that he was becoming attached to her.

Rifke thought of what Willem had said. Being a mother. The possessiveness that made Ma so fierce was not so different from Izula's. And Ma's jealousy of Aunty – that must have begun to simmer when they were children. It had turned into a poisonous seething that had frothed and bubbled from the time Mirele went to live in Kimberley, and had boiled over with the red dress that Aunty had bought her.

Rifke drew a deep breath that made her shudder. If only she could reel back time, back to that moment when Aunty reached to do up the hooks and eyes at the back of the dress. If only Rifke had looked at Ma with softer eyes.

Slowly Rifke unfurled the thought she'd crushed into a ball. Her father was not the elegant, cream-suited man of her fantasies. He was not an enigmatic screen god.

Her father was a drunkard.

Memories stirred like pale ghosts. Shouting that went on for hours. Ma's muffled crying. One day the tall shadowy figure reeled across the living room and the front door slammed. And then he was gone. The flat was quiet. Later, Mirele disappeared too.

Then there were only the two of them left: Ma and Rifke. And Ma enfolded Rifke, holding her tightly every night, her tears rolling hot down Rifke's neck. Sometimes it felt as though Rifke were being smothered.

Rifke rubbed her eyes.

But there was no doubt – Ma loved her. Really loved her. Maybe loved her more than Mirele, because it was Rifke she'd chosen.

'All that she has' Willem had said about Izula and Sibu. The words echoed in Rifke's mind.

She was all that Ma had.

A pain in her chest made her cry out loud. It was as

though someone had dug their hands in and was wrenching her apart. She fell forward, clutching herself, gasping for breath as sobs broke from her.

'Rebecca! What is wrong?' Willem bent over her. He must have come running. He was panting. 'Tell me – what is it? Are you sick? Did something bit you?'

His voice sounded so distant. For a moment she didn't know who he was or where she was.

'Rebecca – if it is a snake we must do something quick! Show me quick where is the bite.'

She shook her head. 'It . . . it . . . isn't . . . a bite.' She spoke through her tears, her body juddering. 'It is – I have . . . just realized – I have done something . . . terrible.' She ground the heels of her hands into her eyes and tried to wipe her nose on her sleeve.

Willem handed her a handkerchief. It smelt of engine oil. 'Rebecca. Shh, shh. Please don't cry like this. Nothing can this bad be.' He spoke quietly.

Rifke held her breath, trying to stop a fresh wave of sobs that swelled and rose and threatened to drown her. Minutes passed. She dragged his handkerchief over her eyes, then looked up at him.

'Yes, Willem. Yes, it is bad. I ran away. I ran away from my mother. I left her alone.' She swallowed more tears. 'All this time I just thought she would be in Johannesburg, waiting for me, living the same life but just without me. But – how can I have been so stupid – stupid and selfish and . . . so cruel – Oh, Willem, she must think that – that I am . . . dead.' She buried her face in her hands.

Willem knelt next to her. He waited for her to calm down again.

'Come, Rebecca. Let us go for a walk.' He looked around the graveyard. 'This is not a happy place to sit.'

A lizard scuttled over her boot. She waited until it had taken shelter under the rock before standing up.

Chapter Thirty-Four

Willem insisted that she go back into the house to fetch the hat. The sun was regaining its confidence after all the rain, and Rifke could feel it trying out its strength on her face again.

He led her away from the main house, past the barns and the dairy and the chicken coop. They walked in silence – a companionable silence. Rifke sensed that Willem didn't want to ask her questions she didn't feel up to answering; at the same time she felt that he would be happy to listen to her. Their boots crunched over the stony track, and the toolbox clanked against Willem's leg. Occasionally Willem pointed out a puddle or a heap of dung she should avoid. His shoulder blades were sharp ridges in his faded shirt, and for a while Rifke concentrated on them. It helped to keep her mind in check.

They stopped outside a couple of sheds. Like everything else at Driemieliesfontein, they were tumbledown and in need of repair. Willem took a hoop of keys out of his pocket. He unlocked the padlock and slid the toolbox through the gap, before locking up again.

'What's in there?' Rifke asked.

Willem coloured and waved his hand vaguely. 'Er . . . they is just some sheds. For storing things.' He glanced at

Rifke. 'There is – I is working on something in there. But I – It is *'n geheim* – a secret.'

Rifke nodded. Just as he hadn't pressed her, she wouldn't press him to tell her his secret.

They walked on. Willem pointed out the stretch of land where grape vines had been laid out, their woody branches stretched like linked shoulders along wires.

'Since Pa went away, the grapes is not doing so good. A long time ago, the grapes is making very good wine. Moeder is finding it . . . difficult to keep everything going.'

'She really depends on you, doesn't she?'

Willem scratched his head and flushed a little. 'We all does what we can. There is no *keuse*. How do you say it?'

'Choice. No choice.'

Willem nodded. Rifke thought he looked wistful.

'If you had a choice, what would you do?'

He stopped.

'Engineer. Grandma spoke to me of the great English engineer, Isambard Kingdom Brunel. I would like one day – it is my dream, maybe I can go to Johannesburg to study.' He looked into the distance for a moment, then looked down. He rubbed the toecap of his right boot against his left trouser leg.

'You could do that. You could go and study engineering.'

Willem sighed and shook his head. 'No, Rebecca. There is not the money. The farm is hard work. We is

barely managing as it is. Even if –when – Pa comes back, we will need still more help.' He looked at Rifke, holding her gaze. 'But it is something I think about every day. I have a little money. Grandma gave it me. It is not much. But it is a start.' He put his hand up. 'You must not tell this – please, Rebecca – to my brothers or to my mother.'

'Of course I won't.' Rifke wondered if whatever he was working on in the shed were part of this dream.

As they carried on walking, Rifke's thoughts kept wheeling back to Ma. Tears threatened her eyes again. She put her hand to her forehead. The hat's straw brim rustled against her fingers. She needed to bring her thoughts back, to distract them.

'What was your grandmother like?' Rifke asked.

For the first time Willem's face relaxed and his eyes shone. 'She is breaking every rule. She talked when she should have been quiet, but she would not speak when she was supposed to. She picked all the flowers in Moeder's garden, but she planted more for her that grew even much more better than Moeder's.' He laughed. 'She played her violin on Sundays because she said it was joyful. When she could not sleep, sometimes she baked cakes in the middle of the night.' He stopped walking and pointed. 'Do you see those trees over there? Grandma showed me and Anton how to climb them. And Piet and Hendrik too. She got up there even not long before she died.'

Rifke tried to imagine straight-backed Mevrou van

Niel living alongside lively Cecily Wainwright, and couldn't. 'Gosh – it couldn't have been easy for your mother – you know, when she married your father and came to live here and she had to find a way to fit in.'

Willem frowned a little. '*Ja*, it was very difficult, I think. Moeder is the daughter of a *predikant* – a preacher, do you say? She has very stiff beliefs. Two strong women in one house – it is the cause of much problems. Moeder is saying that Grandma is interfering, but Grandma says she is only helping. Sometimes when things is very difficult, Grandma is going to live by herself in that little house there over by the railway.' His glasses had slid to the end of his nose. He took them off. 'It is worse when the War is beginning. Never did Grandma forgot she was English. She spoke many times of England. The special green of the grass. The rain which falls softly. Pa is also very proud that he is half-English. But Moeder – she does not want Pa to fight on the side of England.'

Rifke sighed. How easy it was to make quick judgements, and how often they turned out to be unbalanced, or not exactly true or, as she was discovering, just plain wrong. Cecily Wainwright was nothing like how she'd imagined. Mevrou's life on the farm was not straightforward. Rifke had trusted Anton and despised Willem. She didn't even want to begin to think about Ma and Aunty and her father.

'So,' Rifke said, after a minute or two, 'your grandmother taught you English?'

'*Ja*, she tried, Rebecca.' He grinned, pushing his glasses back on. 'But maybe she didn't have such good students. My English is *swak* – weak.' Willem's voice was soft and he spoke carefully. She liked the way small lines like brackets appeared at the side of his mouth when he smiled.

'No, it's not. Really it's not. Anyway, how can you expect to speak fluent English when there's no one around to speak English with?'

She thought of Ma. Nineteen years in South Africa. Lots of people around her speaking English. And still she stumbled and faltered. Maybe it wasn't that easy after all.

They were passing the vineyards. The farm seemed to go on forever. It was getting even hotter, and the air was humming. Rifke swatted at the cloud of midges that hung around her head, sometimes flying right into her nostrils.

The ground sloped downwards and became marshy. Rifke could hear the rush of water. It was greener here, with denser bushes and high reeds, and soon they found themselves standing on the bank of a furious river. In some places, it was boiling up rocks and brown sludge, and in others it was thrusting branches and twigs down-stream.

'In a few days it will calm down. Then here is a good place to swim.' Willem wiped his forehead on his sleeve. He pointed to a flat piece of rock. 'It is a good place also to sit.'

The stone was warm, while the fine spray coming off the water was cool. Rifke allowed the roar of the water to drown out her thoughts. Willem was right. It was a good place to sit. She looked at him out of the corner of her eye. He sat very still beside her, his long fingers resting on his knees. How could she have misjudged him so?

Chapter Thirty-Five

Rifke reached for the calendar beside her bed. She scratched out Wednesday, 2nd February. Three days to go. Never before had she wished that time would pass as quickly as she did now. Not even during school exams. She was even looking forward to the Chrysmol!

Out of the corner of her eye, Rifke could see the wooden Jesus hanging on the wall. After she'd moved the bed away from the rain, she'd left the bed in its new position. It was a compromise: taking the crucifix down might have offended Mevrou van Niel, but remaining under it would definitely have upset Ma. Rifke closed her eyes. She recited the prayer Ma always said on getting up in the morning. Tears sprang up when she found herself fumbling for some of the words.

There was a rustle as something was slipped under her door. Rifke got out of bed. A note. She recognized the brown paper: some of the stuff in the crate had been wrapped in it, and most of it had been cut up for lavatory paper. Quickly she scanned the message:

I must do something but when I is finished about one o'clock do you want to swim in the river? It is calm now. If yes I will wait for you outside the sheds (secret). Willem.

Rifke unlocked the door as fast as she could. She darted into the passage and looked both ways. He wasn't there. She'd hardly seen him since the day he'd taken her down to the river. She'd had to spend the last few days shadowing Mevrou van Niel, always checking, constantly nervous, in case Anton appeared.

Rifke ran her finger over Willem's writing. It was spindly and angular, just like him. He reminded her of a young giraffe she'd seen at Johannesburg Zoo – gawky and shy, with long eyelashes, slightly out of control, all elbows and knees. She folded his note and put it into her pocket. It wasn't just his protection she wanted; she liked talking to him. She thought about his invitation. The river would be lovely and fresh. But her heart sank – just as she would if she got into the water. She couldn't swim. Why hadn't she listened when Mirele had tried to teach her at Muizenberg? Rifke hadn't liked the tug of the sea, and she'd only allowed the water to lick her ankles before running out to seek refuge with Uncle Ber under the umbrella. And even if she'd known how to swim, there was still the problem of a bathing costume. Of course she didn't have one, and after her experience with Mevrou's brassiere there was no way she was going to ask to borrow hers.

When Rifke walked into the kitchen, Mevrou van Niel was just on her way out. Her soft hat was pulled down

over her head, and over her arms and in her hands she bore a selection of baskets and buckets.

'Coffee is warm, Rebecca.' She gestured at the metal pot. The buckets clanked. 'I is going now. The *bessies* – berries is now ripe. I must them pick.'

Hendrik and Piet were already outside. Rifke could hear them whooping as they kicked a ball around. Mevrou left the room. Rifke panicked. No way was she going to be left behind. If Anton appeared . . . She sloshed a bit of coffee into a cup, gulped it down and ran outside.

Sibu was in the garden, chasing the ball Piet and Hendrik had abandoned.

'Sibu!'

He looked up, then ran towards her. She put her arms out and he ran into them, laughing.

'Sibu, you're better!' She swung him around a few times until he shrieked. 'Let me see your ears,' she said in Afrikaans. He held himself very still as she looked at them. The bone discs were still in place, but the earlobes didn't look so bad. A bit scabby, but not bleeding and leaking pus as they had been.

'I've got to go now,' she said, and tried to set him down.

He giggled and clung on to her even more tightly. She loved the way his cheek felt so smooth and soft against hers. If only she could take him with her to pick berries.

Rifke glanced around. No sign of Izula. She held on to Sibu and hurried along.

They were passing Willem's sheds. 'I think I'll just pop in and tell Willem that I won't be able to go swimming,' she murmured.

'Willem?' Sibu asked. It must have been the only word he'd recognized.

'*Ja. Oom Willem,*' she said with a smile. It was strange to think of Willem as Sibu's uncle. Uncles were usually like Uncle Ber: portly and balding and suffering from dyspepsia.

The shed doors were shut. Rifke knocked as loudly as she could so that he would hear her above the banging coming from inside.

'Willem!' she called.

The hammering stopped. Willem came to the door. He opened it only a couple of inches, before sliding out. He blinked in the bright sunshine. There was a stripe of grease across his forehead.

Rifke grinned, and he grinned back.

'Hello, Rebecca! But –' he looked at his watch – 'it is not yet one o'clock.'

'Yes, no, I'm sorry, Willem. It's just – well, I can't go swimming.' She blushed. 'I haven't got a costume.'

He nodded and wiped his hands on his trousers. 'One minute, Rebecca.' He disappeared into the shed again, only to reappear a minute later with a basket.

'What's in here?' she asked. Sibu leaned across her and

224

tried to poke in it. 'Sibu – please let me put you down,' she said in Afrikaans. Willem reached out and lifted Sibu away from her.

'*Oom!*' Sibu said. Willem frowned for a second, but then, to Rifke's relief, he laughed.

There was a towel at the top of the basket. Rifke took it out. Underneath was a black costume.

'I think maybe it is not big, not small for you, Rebecca. Grandma is – was – your size.'

For a moment Rifke wavered. Cecily Wainwright's bedroom. Her hat. And now her swimming costume. But Willem was looking at her expectantly. And it was already so hot; sweat was trickling down her back. Oh, why not? Soon she'd be gone, she thought again. There was no way she was going to turn into Cecily Wainwright, stuck in Driemieliesfontein forever.

She smiled. 'Thank you, Willem.' She put the costume and towel back into the basket and put it over her arm. 'Um – there is another problem.' She looked up at him, blushing again. 'I . . . er . . . can't swim.'

'Don't worry, Rebecca,' he said with a grin. 'Now the river is calm, and the water – it is not deep. You can try. If you is – are – not happy, it does not matter. You can just put your toes in.' He pushed his glasses back into position. 'And I will look after you,' he added softly.

Chapter Thirty-Six

Rifke changed into Cecily Wainwright's swimming costume behind a clump of reeds.

The costume was old-fashioned: it had a skirt with built-in shorts. At least twenty years old, she guessed. But it fitted, and it wasn't made of heavy wool like Ma and Aunty's costumes. They said the wool didn't go transparent in the water – but it might as well have, because when wet the costumes absorbed half the Atlantic Ocean and sagged against Ma and Aunty's ample bodies, advertising every single roll and pouch of flesh. Rifke smiled at the thought of Muizenberg's finest ladies, and those who weren't so fine, all made equal by their heavy, dragged-down swimwear.

Willem had changed into his swimming trunks and was already in the water.

'Is all right – Grandma's *baaikostuum*?' he asked.

'Yes, thank you. It's a perfect fit,' Rifke said. She sat down on the bank. The water *was* calm; it dawdled past, crystal clear and sparkling in the afternoon sunshine. She dipped her feet in. Cold! Her toes curled with surprise.

Willem had been sitting on the riverbed. When he stood up, Rifke could see that the water didn't even reach his knees. He waded towards her.

'It is not deep here, Rebecca,' he said.

'I'm – um, I'm sorry, Willem. I'm a bit nervous.' Rifke hugged herself.

'There is no hurry.'

Slowly, and with lots of encouragement from Willem, Rifke eased herself into the river until they both were sitting in the middle of the water. She even felt brave enough to lie back until her hair floated like waterweed behind her. It was delicious being half hot and half cool, and she laughed out loud with the joy of it.

When their fingers and toes turned into prunes, they clambered back on to the riverbank and lay head to head on their towels. Rifke loved the way a light breeze on her warm skin felt like silk being wafted over her. The way the red dress had felt when she'd let it swirl around her that afternoon a hundred years ago. She closed her eyes. When she opened them, Willem was resting his chin on his hands, looking at her and frowning.

'I – It is not long – until you is going,' he said.

'Three days. I'll be going in three days.' She felt a surge of excitement mixed with panic. 'I can't wait to see my mother again.' Her voice caught and she squeezed her eyes shut. Whatever it took, she had to get on that train and find her way back to Johannesburg.

'What time will the train come on Sunday, Willem?' He didn't reply.

'Willem?' A cold shadow fell across her face. She opened her eyes.

'This is very, very cosy.' It was Anton, standing over them. He had a rifle in his hands. When he swayed a little, the stark sunlight behind him blinded Rifke. Her heart pounded. She fumbled at her towel to cover herself, but she couldn't see properly.

'What do you want?' Willem said in Afrikaans, standing up. 'Clear off!'

At last Rifke freed the towel and scrabbled to wrap herself in it, but not before Anton trawled a look over her body. He poked Willem in the chest with the butt of the rifle and, throwing his head back, he gave a dry laugh.

Willem shoved the rifle away. 'Get lost!' he said, his voice rising.

'Listen, Rebecca! *Hy skreeu soos 'n maer vark!* How you say? – He screams like a pig. And I thought you Jewish doesn't like pigs.'

Rifke couldn't speak. Couldn't bear to meet his eyes. Why didn't he just go?

She heard him laugh again, then whistle through his fingers the way their netball teacher did at school. One sharp note.

'Leeu!' Anton shouted.

Rifke froze. The dog was on the other side of the riverbank. There was something bloody and furry clamped in his jaws. Some sort of rabbit, still twitching. The dog stared at Rifke.

'It's all right, Rebecca.' Willem drew her away. 'Leeu

228

– he is more interested in that *dassie* than in you. Don't look at him.'

Rifke shuddered and drew the towel more closely around her.

'Can we – Do you mind if we go back now?' she asked Willem.

Willem looked over his shoulder, narrowing his eyes. Rifke turned too, and they both watched Anton striding off. The dog bounded down the bank and through the water. The musty smell of blood and death hit Rifke's nostrils as he passed her.

'*Ja*, Rebecca. Let us go back. Anton has spoilt the afternoon. Just like he spoils everything.' He bent to collect his clothes. 'I hate him,' he muttered, so softly Rifke almost didn't hear it.

Chapter Thirty-Seven

Anton's shadow stayed over Rifke – and not just for the rest of that afternoon. It mingled with her increasing desperation to get away from Driemieliesfontein, to get back to Johannesburg and back to Ma. Her stomach churned and she barely slept. Counting down the hours, she bit her nails to the quick, then turned her restless teeth on the skin around them.

Early on Saturday, Piet and Hendrik carried the berries from the cold room under the dairy into the kitchen. The house filled with their sweet scent.

'The berries won't last long in this weather,' Mevrou van Niel said at the breakfast table. She spoke in Afrikaans to her two younger sons; they and Rifke were the only ones left in the house.

'I hate making jam,' Piet groaned. 'Can't I do something else?'

'*Ja*, it's much too hot,' Hendrik said. 'I'd rather clean out the pigsty than make jam. Why can't we just eat some of the berries and feed the rest to the pigs?'

Mevrou van Niel twisted a few stray fronds of hair and threaded them back into her bun. She turned her wedding band a few times, then reached for the dirty plates.

'Every year it is the same. I do not need to answer that.'

Rifke cleared her throat. 'I will help you. I know how to make jam.' Being busy might take some of the edge off her jumpiness. And it would help bring Sunday round more quickly.

Mevrou turned her green-eyed gaze on Rifke. She'd become even more distant since Willem had told her about Anton attacking Rifke.

She took a moment to consider Rifke's offer. 'Thank you,' she said, and turned her back as she carried the crockery to the sink. 'And Piet, Hendrik –' she looked over her shoulder – 'you boys will clean out the pigsty. The cow shed too.'

All day Rifke and Mevrou stirred the pots of bubbling fruit and sweated as they stirred. The day ground slowly by as jar after jar was filled, and they hardly exchanged a word. Rifke was wondering whether Mevrou even realized she would be leaving the next day, when Mevrou put down the wooden spoon and turned to her.

'It is the train tomorrow, *ja*?' she said.

Rifke nodded.

'The train – it is usually arriving at eleven o'clock in the morning. It is about one hour and a half to walk to the station.'

'So I will leave here at nine – to be sure to get there on time?'

Mevrou nodded. 'Quarter past nine is also fine.' She wiped her palms on her apron and looked down.

Rifke wondered if she might say something – something about what a pleasure it had been to have another female presence in the house, or an extra pair of hands. She said nothing.

Rifke glanced at Mevrou. Rifke was not sad to be leaving Driemieliesfontein. Still, even though Mevrou was strange in her stiff-backed, rigid ways, imagine if she hadn't allowed Rifke to stay. Goose pimples rose on Rifke's skin – Ma would be right to be mourning her now.

'Mevrou van Niel.' Rifke's voice came out in a whisper. 'Mevrou van Niel,' she repeated, more loudly.

Mevrou looked up.

'I want to say . . . thank you,' Rifke said. 'For – for everything.'

Mevrou looked startled, and then, for the first time in the whole month, she smiled. It was a shy smile, and it didn't last long. It made her look remarkably like Willem. She nodded and turned back to the pot she was scraping out.

After dinner, Mevrou helped her fill the bathtub with warm water. Scrubbing away at her skin, Rifke felt as though she were washing away her month at Driemieliesfontein. It fed her impatience to get away. That night, Rifke did not sleep at all.

She was upset too, and surprised to feel so upset:

Willem hadn't appeared all day. He hadn't come in for dinner, and no one had said why he wasn't there. Would she see him at all before she left?

Part Three

Part Three

Chapter Thirty-Eight

The dress Rifke had arrived in was now a washed-out and limp relic. It seemed to have shrunk too. Rifke put it on and buckled her sandals. She moved the bed back to its position under the crucifix, then took the blue canvas bag off the door handle. From the kitchen she could smell coffee. Perhaps Willem was there. She left the bedroom without looking back.

'It is very early,' Mevrou said.

She was in her Sunday clothes. Piet and Hendrik were sitting at the table, rustling in their best trousers and shirts. Willem's place was not even set. There was no sign of him.

'I – I couldn't sleep. I don't want to miss the train,' Rifke said.

Mevrou had made strong coffee. Its burnt smell mingled with the sweet scent of the jam they'd made the day before and the swirl of nervous acid in her stomach. It made Rifke feel sick. She perched on a chair and turned her head away from the food set out on the table.

Mevrou approached Rifke. She was holding a brown-paper package and a glass bottle.

'Rebecca, here is some sandwiches. There is also some apples and a bottle with water.'

'Thank you, Mevrou.' Rifke took the package. It was heavy. How long did Mevrou think she would be travelling, for goodness sake? But she knew Ma would have done exactly the same, and it made her smile. She put the package and the bottle in her bag.

Mevrou finished washing the plates and dried her hands. She fetched her special bonnet out of the laundry and called Piet and Hendrik to attention.

'Time for church,' she said, tying the ribbons under her chin.

Rifke stood up. She couldn't bear it any longer. 'Where is Willem, please?'

'Anton sent word with – with the girl for him to go up to the boundary. Anton is needing help there,' Mevrou said. 'Willem will not be here for two, maybe three days.' There wasn't a hint of apology in her voice, nor any suggestion that Willem might have sent a goodbye message.

Rifke felt hurt spread like a bruise after a blow. Anger too. At Anton for spoiling things again. At Mevrou for turning a blind eye. And, most of all, at Willem for letting her down. She turned away and blinked back her tears. It was time to go. She hoisted the canvas bag over her arm.

Mevrou moved towards her and took her hand. 'Goodbye, Rebecca.' Her fingers were cold and Rifke could feel the calluses rasping against her own skin. 'I wish you *baie* . . . very luck.'

'Goodbye, Mevrou. Thank you again. Bye, Piet. Bye, Hendrik. *Totsiens*.'

The boys nudged each other and laughed, then under their mother's watchful eye they said goodbye in Afrikaans.

Rifke shut the garden door behind her for the last time, then the garden gate, closing off her month at Driemieliesfontein. There was one other person she really wanted to see. She made her way towards the outbuildings, stepping over the white animal bones Sibu liked to play with.

'Sibu!' Rifke called. She waited, but there was no sound, no sign of anyone inside. 'Sibu!' she called again.

Still nothing. She would have to leave without seeing either Willem or Sibu. Tears rose in her eyes again, and she dashed them away on her sleeve.

She hurried down the drive, retracing the steps she'd made the month before. Never ever again did she want to find herself in the depths of the veld. Looking at it through a train window would be enough – more than enough.

It wasn't long before she left the drive and joined the sandy path leading away from Driemieliesfontein and towards the station. As her feet scuffed their way through the dry soil, her head was already finding its way down Eloff Street. The eucalyptus trees became Johannesburg's tall buildings and the hum of the insects were the motorbikes that buzzed down the avenues.

A child cried out. It took Rifke a moment or two to call herself back to her surroundings.

'Sibu?' she said, stopping and looking around.

Ahead of her on her left was the derelict cottage she'd spotted when she arrived, the cottage where Cecily Wainwright had sometimes taken refuge. She'd walked further than she'd realized; she wasn't far from the station. There was no sign of Sibu. Perhaps she'd imagined the cry. She moved the bag on to her other arm and set off again.

As she drew level with the abandoned cottage, a howl of pain stopped her in her tracks. The voice was unmistakable.

'Sibu!' She turned off the path and blundered through the bushes, beating branches and twigs away from her eyes.

The undergrowth was trampled down in front of the cottage, and the door was ajar. She flung it fully open and ran straight into a fire-blackened room. It smelt of damp and charcoal and absence. Rifke darted through and into the adjacent room. Mottled light filtered first through the trees and then through the tiny windowpanes. The rooms were empty apart from charred furniture, still arranged as it must have been when Cecily Wainwright lived there.

There was a whine and a click, a gust of air followed by stillness. Rifke looked over her shoulder. The front door had closed. But it wasn't windy – so why would it have swung shut? Perhaps Sibu was playing a game. She

turned back to the entrance. Rifke heard a voice, muffled, stifled rather, like someone playing hide and seek. And the grinding of a key in the lock.

'Sibu – make open!' she called out in Afrikaans, banging on the door which, she soon realized, was most definitely locked. She twisted the inside handle and pulled and rattled with all her strength.

'Sibu!' she shouted again.

But then it occurred to her that there was no way Sibu could lock a door. Running to the window, she was just in time to catch sight of two people, their backs to her, running away from the house.

Anton and Izula. Three people – for Rifke now noticed Sibu, who was tied to Izula's back in a red blanket, his arms flailing about.

Rifke pounded on the window. 'Open the door! Let me out!' She leaped on to the sill and clawed at the catch, putting all her weight behind the frame as she tried to heave it up. It was no use. Rifke could see the shiny new screws, securing it shut. She pressed her face to the corner of the window and smacked her palms against the glass until they stung.

'Let me out!' she screamed.

Izula leaned into Anton. They both turned at the same time. Their faces were masks, each a leer of evil glee.

Then Anton broke away and made for the window. He staggered against it and angled himself until his face was level with Rifke's. She heard his ragged laugh before he flattened his face against the glass, first his nose, then his eye – bloodshot, wide-pupilled – then his mouth, the stubble around the lips scratching through the film of condensing breath. Rifke stepped backwards, repelled.

'*Ja!*' he shouted, his voice distorted. He rubbed at the glass with the side of his hand. Rifke saw the glow of the end of a roughly rolled cigarette. He took a deep drag. His eyes rolled backwards for an instant.

'Just open the damn door, will you!' Rifke screamed.

'Didn't I told you, Rebecca . . . you must watch out?' His speech was halting, and blurred. 'Like my grand-mother . . . you didn't know when you came here . . . you will be staying here – until you die!'

Rifke felt panic burn in her chest. Anton laughed again and stubbed the cigarette against the glass. Izula approached, unsteady too.

'Please, Izula – open the door!' Rifke shouted in Afrikaans.

Izula turned her head away, but not before Rifke caught sight of a sideways look that was hesitant, a bit uncertain.

'Rest in peace!' Anton hissed through the windowpane and drawing himself to his full height, he rested a hand on Izula's shoulder. She glanced up at him, then at Rifke, and her look this time was triumphant.

They lurched away, crashing into bushes. Rifke darted to the other window. Izula's blanket flashed among the greens and greys of the dense foliage. Anton flung his

arm into the air. His fisted hand rose and opened, and something small and silver twisted in the sunlight, flaring briefly before dropping into the undergrowth.

The key.

'No!' Rifke shouted. The word died in her throat as the red scraps of blanket disappeared completely. Anton and Izula wouldn't come back; she was certain of that.

Rifke remembered the hammerhead bird. A storm and a death. That's what Piet or Hendrik had said it meant – and the storm part had certainly come true.

She began to shudder and sweat. No one else knew she was here. Willem and Piet and Hendrik and Mevrou – they all thought she'd gone, taken the train back to Johannesburg.

Her heart jackhammering in her chest, she ran through the rooms, looking to see if there was a back door or some other way to get out. There wasn't. She pulled and shoved and rattled at the front door. It remained obstinately shut. The door was thick and the lock was new. She could smash the windows. But the panes were smaller than her hands, and only an axe could bash through the sturdy wooden bars. Sobs threatened the back of her throat.

'No point in crying,' she said out loud, swallowing hard. 'Come on, come on.'

She raced through the two rooms, beating on the walls. The smaller room was a bedroom; the larger held a dining table, a couple of dining chairs and a small sofa.

Rifke's fevered gaze barely took in the candlesticks on the table or the tray still set for tea with delicate china. It was hot in the house. The sun was pounding on the low tin roof. Sweat pooled in her armpits and trickled down her face and back. She pulled her cardigan off and stuffed it in the bag.

'Got to get out of here,' she muttered. 'Got to get on that train. Quick. Quick.' Her voice was dry in her throat. Faster and faster she paced the rooms, maddened with heat and despair. Then she tripped over some boxes strewn across the floor.

Chapter Thirty-Nine

It took a few seconds before she registered the puddle of cold liquid under her right knee. And a few more before she looked up and spotted the hole in the corrugated roof. A ragged, burnt-edged opening about the size of an ink-pot lid. Thank goodness for the storm – if it hadn't been for the rain coming through the roof, she'd never have spotted the hole. Rifke stood up, breathing heavily. Could she make it bigger? Big enough to climb through?

A faint tremor passed under her feet – no more than a tremble at first, a hum that was almost unnoticeable. Rifke looked around for something to poke at the hole with. Just then the teacups began to shiver on the tray, tinkling politely on their saucers.

'W-what?' Rifke stiffened. 'What's that?' And then it dawned on her.

The train.

Dragging the table to where she'd been kneeling, she scrambled on to it. She could only just reach the roof, scraping it with her scrabbling fingertips. She leaped down, threw one of the chairs on to the table and climbed up again. Using the chair legs, she bashed at the roof, heart pounding, panting, sweating and half sobbing.

Burnt iron crumbled and flaked and fell into her hair and open mouth.

The far-off ring of metal against metal. A long, tinny whistle.

Rifke grabbed the canvas bag and slung it over her arm. Setting the chair back on to its legs, she clambered on to it. It skated a bit on the table surface. She caught the jagged edge of the hole in the roof with one hand, barely noticing the searing hot metal.

Head and shoulders out of the house. Sun on her head. Plume of steam. Coming closer.

She flung the bag out. Heard it slide down the roof's slant. Her turn next. She pressed both hands on the edge of the metal and climbed slowly up the chair's ladder-back.

Crump. The sound of metal cracking.

No. Please no.

No time to think about it. Just go. With one heavy push, she jackknifed her legs against the chair. It rocked on the table top, snared her foot between the bars of its ladder-back and began to pull her down.

'No!' she screamed. She kicked her foot free. Felt the chair skid away, and then she was holding on to crumbling corrugated tin, her legs cycling in air. Smacking and grabbing the roof, she edged herself forward until the rest of her body flipped on to the metal and she felt herself sliding headfirst downwards. And off the edge.

A bush caught her. Pulling herself free of its grasp, she didn't hear it tear her dress or feel its thorns. Snatching up the canvas bag, she ran.

Chapter Forty

Above the trees and scrub, the train's steam billowed. Rifke flew towards it. One word formed in her head and she found herself shouting it in time with the train's rhythm. 'Ma . . . Ma . . . Ma . . .' Twice she fell, the soles of her sandals too smooth to grip the shifting ochre earth. Tiny stones cut her hands and knees.

The heaving of the train's engine filled the air. It was very close. Rifke could hear its high squeal soften to a sigh.

She burst out of the scrub into the open.

It was there! The train was there! Just an engine again, drawing into the station, panting, slowing.

Every sinew in her body – her lungs, her eyes, the soles of her feet – all burning, Rifke hurled herself through the twenty or so feet between herself and the station embankment . . . just as the train sucked in a deep breath and, with a shudder and hiss, gathered its strength again.

'No!' A scream tore from Rifke's throat. The train was moving.

She flung herself against the embankment, clutching, frantic.

The roar and clank and grinding of the pistons and

wheels, and the gush and whoosh of steam, almost drowned the short chirrup of the guard's whistle.

'Stop! Wait!' Rifke yelled. 'Wait for me!' She pulled herself on to the platform, arms and legs crabbed. Staggered to her feet, dragging the bag.

The train kept moving.

In the shimmering light it was hard to gauge its distance. Time slowed; like syrup pulled with a spoon from a tin, it hung in a liquid festoon, and Rifke felt as though she had forever to reach the train and hook her hands on to the handle at its rear and leap aboard its small ledge. Dropping the bag, she ran, her arms wheeling, her mouth open in a silent cry.

The train pulled free of the station.

Gone.

Rifke's legs carried her forwards, unable to stop, until the platform ran out and there was just the railway line, still ringing with the train's vibrations. Her legs buckled and she skidded to her knees.

'Ma . . . Ma . . .' she sobbed. She'd been within touching distance of home, and now it felt as though Ma had gone, departed with the train, far beyond her reach.

Another month before the next train. The horror of it filled her like a poisonous gas. Gasping for air through the sobs that wracked her chest, she watched the engine shrink to a grey dot, and disappear.

Chapter Forty-One

She became suddenly aware of the grating of sand beneath shoes. Someone was running up behind her. She stiffened. Not Anton. Please not Anton.

'Rebecca!'

She turned. She had to wipe her eyes on her arm to see clearly.

'Willem?' Her voice came out in shudders.

'Rebecca – thank goodness. The train is not here yet. I am in time.' He was panting. 'I wanted to say goodbye to you.' He bent over, resting a hand on each knee, trying to catch his breath. His hair was dark with sweat, his shirt plastered to his back.

Seeing him, hearing his soft voice, so pleased, made Rifke begin to cry all over again. She covered her face with her palms and turned away, heaving with sobs.

'Rebecca, what is it? What is wrong?' Willem touched her shoulder. 'Oh my goodness, Rebecca – what has happened to you? You is covered in cuts and black stuff and your dress is torn!'

Rifke took a few deep breaths, trying to still her tears. 'The train – it's g-gone. Anton and Izula – they tr-trapped me. I m-missed the train.'

250

'What? The train is already gone?' His face clouded. 'Anton has hurt you?'

He put one long, gentle hand to the side of her face and she found herself leaning against it as she told him in halting bursts what had happened.

'I hate him!' he shouted, pulling away from her. 'I hate him with every . . . every cell in my body.' He tightened his trembling hands into fists and held his arms stiffly at the sides of his body.

Rifke wiped her eyes, and looking up into Willem's face she saw that he'd been hurt. She pointed to the drops of blood leaking down his cheek. 'Th-there's blood.' There was also a bruise along his jaw, and one of the lenses of his glasses was cracked.

He put one of his fists to his face and dashed at the cut in an angry, dismissive gesture. 'Why did I let him trick me? I know him. I know what he is like. And still I went there. All the way up to the border to fix the fence I knew I already fixed very good.' He tensed his fists again. '*Hy't my bewusteloos geklap* – how do you say it? – he punched me unconscious and . . . and he tied me up so I is not able to get away. I did not know why he is doing this to me.' Willem took a sharp breath. 'Now I understand. Anton planned all this. He knew when you is wanting to take the train, Rebecca. That you is wanting to go back to your mother.'

At the mention of her mother, Rifke's eyes filled with tears again. She felt suddenly exhausted, small in this wide, hot landscape, defenceless and weak and drained of any wish to fight on. She rested her head on her knees. A raw cawing overhead echoed in the stagnant air. Probably another hammerhead, Rifke thought, without looking up. The Angel of Death, more likely, bypassing the Angel of Sickness altogether. Maybe the hammerhead and the Angel of Death were one and the same. The contents of Ma's special suitcase would be useless now.

'Rebecca.' She felt Willem sit down beside her. His bony elbow knocked against her arm. 'Come with me. It will be all right, Rebecca.'

Rifke's head swirled. It took a while for Willem's voice to clot into words she could understand. 'No, it won't. Nothing will ever be all right again.' She flapped her hand. 'Go away.' She wasn't going back to Driemielies-fontein. She would rather sit out here until she withered like a dry leaf and the wind came off the mountains and blew her off the edge of Africa and into the sea.

'No, listen to me. *Ek dink* – I think it is possible – I can take you away from here.'

Rifke shook her head. She remained silent. Where did he think he could take her? There was nothing for miles. Too much effort to go somewhere else and die of thirst and starvation and exhaustion in the process. Dying just where she was would be fine.

Willem made an impatient noise. He stood up. Rifke felt the cool of his shadow over her.

'Stand up!'

252

She'd never heard him speak like that to her. She lifted her head. He looked half cross and half amused. He bent down and took her hands.

'Please get up, Rebecca.' He pulled her to her feet. 'You remember my secret? I will show you what I has been working on. It is how I can help you get back to your family.' He tugged her arm. Too worn out to resist, she allowed him to drag her down the platform.

Chapter Forty-Two

Willem led Rifke back towards the farm. They walked slowly, taking it in turns to swig from the bottle of water from Rifke's bag.

He knew without her saying anything that she didn't want to go near the house again, so they took a path from the station that curved away from Driemieliesfontein. They emerged from a cluster of bushes behind the shed in which Willem tended his secret – whatever that was. Rifke was past caring.

The keys jangled as he unlocked the doors, jarring the cannonball that was already rolling around inside her head.

'Come in, Rebecca. Quick.'

Willem shut the doors behind her. It was more a barn than a shed. Light slanted in from two huge windows in the roof. It was hot. Rifke sniffed. The air was dry and it smelt of engine oil. In the centre of the room, there was a large mound covered in grubby cloths. Willem was grinning and pointing at it.

'What? What is it?' Rifke frowned, holding her head.

Willem pulled at the cloths. They slid off to reveal a rust-coloured old pick-up truck, the bonnet a bit dented. She looked away. So what? It was just a truck. A truck that couldn't go anywhere. Anton had made that clear to her when she'd first arrived. Was Willem teasing her? If so, it wasn't funny.

Willem gave the fender or radiator or whatever it was called a little rub with his finger.

'I has been working on the truck for a long time.' He pushed his hair away from his face. The wound on his cheek had stopped leaking blood. '*Ja*, one week or two ago, I made the part I needed from a bit of the engine I took out of the tractor. I has been testing it and testing it.' He rubbed his chin. 'I – I . . . got it to work, Rebecca!'

He looked so happy Rifke had to smile. She still didn't know how a truck could go without petrol – but it seemed mean-spirited to mention something so obvious.

'*Ja*, it's a . . . a lovely truck,' she said, and leaned forward to give it a friendly tap. It hurt her head to move, and she let out an involuntary moan.

Willem sprang to her side, knocking over a pile of old tyres. 'I know, Rebecca, how much you is wanting to go home.' He touched her arm. 'This is my idea. Climb in, Rebecca,' he said, opening the passenger door. 'I was going to have a tryout of the engine one night-time. But . . . why not now? If we start soon, we can get to Johannesburg by the morning. I think – I hope – it will stay working.'

'What? Drive it? Drive the truck? To Johannesburg?'

'*Ja*.' His glasses winked in the sunlight.

'But what about petrol? Anton told me there wasn't any.'

'Anton!' Willem gave a dry laugh. 'He doesn't know as much as he thinks he does.' He grinned at her. 'Don't worry, Rebecca. I have some petrol saved.'

Rifke climbed on to the ledge at the passenger's side of the vehicle, the running board, then hoisted herself into the cabin. The seat was springy, and as she bounced on to it, it gave off a strong smell of old leather – just like Uncle Ber's car. The memory snagged at her heart.

Willem then leaped on to the running board next to her. He leant in through the open door and beamed at her. The sunlight caught his long eyelashes and the mixture of freckles and sunburn across his nose. 'I won't be long, Rebecca. I must now fetch a few things.' His voice caught with excitement. 'Don't worry. We will be gone very, very soon.'

The seat was long, a continuous stretch like a bench. Rifke sat for a minute or two, staring at nothing through the front window, then lay down and closed her eyes. She was going home. The leather was surprisingly cool against her cheek. Calm settled over her. Going home. To Ma.

The roar of the engine woke her. She lurched upright, gripping the edge of the seat.

'We's free! *Ons is vry!*' Willem shouted. His voice rose and broke with joy as they burst through the shed's open doors. Rifke laughed.

Chapter Forty-Three

The dirt track gave way to gravel and finally to a tarred road, and it became easier to speak and be heard.

'You all right, Rebecca?'

She was watching the white lines in the centre of the road. It looked as though the truck were swallowing them, gulping them down until there would be none left and she would be with Ma once more.

Rifke turned to Willem and nodded. He'd opened his window, and the breeze fingered his hair.

'*Ja*, I'm fine,' she said. 'My headache's almost gone.'

'There's some food. There by your feet.'

She'd noticed the hessian sack and wondered what was in it. She unwrapped a stack of sandwiches stuffed into the top.

'Who – Did your mother make these?'

'No. It was I. Moeder does not know I am driving you. No one saw me.' He smiled.

Rifke took a bite of a sandwich. It tasted good.

'Thank you, Willem.' She turned to him. 'Thank you for . . . you know –'

'That is all right.' He cleared his throat. 'Um – I is – am – really – a bit happy you missed the train, Rebecca. S-so I can spend this time with you.'

Rifke felt a blush heat her face, and when she looked across at Willem she saw that he was flushed too. With his eyes fixed on the road ahead, he took his left hand off the steering wheel and placed it on the seat beside him. Suddenly shy, Rifke set her hand into his, and when his fingers curled around hers, she felt a surge of happiness.

Neither said anything. The road was straight, and there were no other vehicles. They drove with their hands entwined, the buzz of the engine as soothing to Rifke as a psalm.

The afternoon sun began to collapse into a molten sunset. It filled the truck with its pink glow. Willem flicked a glance at the dials in the dashboard and frowned.

'What's wrong?' Rifke asked.

'We must stop at the next town. For more petrol. The tank is running low. I put in all I had hidden away from – from Anton.'

They hadn't passed many towns – only abandoned vestiges: the odd advertising hoarding, sun-bleached and peeling, a few burnt-out cars, roofless houses and, sometimes, clusters of huts in the distance.

A knot tightened in Rifke's stomach. 'Will we find a petrol station?'

Willem squeezed her hand. 'I did not want to worry you. It will be fine.' He sounded breezy, but, even in the ebbing light, Rifke could see he was still frowning, and his hand in hers had tensed.

Night rushed in after dusk. Rifke tried not to keep looking at the petrol dial. She bent her mind to wondering what she and Ma would have been doing then if Rifke had been at home. Sitting at the table in the kitchen, most probably, with the faded tablecloth that had come with Ma from Lithuania scratching Rifke's knees. Ma always starched it, even though it was thin and mended in places. Lamb chops and peas for dinner, followed by an apple that Ma insisted on peeling for Rifke, the skin coiling down from the small sharp knife in one long, unbroken piece. Ruthie said if you slung the peel over your shoulder it would form the first letter of your husband-to-be's name. Rifke had a funny thought. She glanced at Willem. Could the peel form a *W*? Her fingers tingled and she shivered a bit.

'You is – are cold,' he said. 'There is a blanket in the bag.'

Rifke pulled it out and spread it over her knees and over Willem's too. His smile was reflected in the dark windscreen. They were alone on the motorway; theirs were the only headlights, boring like cat's eyes through the darkness. If she hadn't been so worried about the petrol, it would have felt cosy.

Again, Rifke swerved her mind. On a Sunday night after dinner, Rifke would finish off her homework, and Ma would knit – something for the soldiers away fighting, a cardigan for either Rifke or herself, or another pair of the argyle socks Rifke wore with her lace-ups. The

Leibowitzes' gramophone started up every night at half past eight on the dot, and Ma would whack the wall with the broom handle and yell at them to turn it off. So embarrassing, especially as Mr Leibowitz took her for music at school. Out on the street the trams would be clanging, their bells ringing tinnily and more audibly as the cars and buses retired for the night, and then stopping altogether at midnight.

All at once, Rifke felt she wanted to talk about Johannesburg, about living in the city and, most of all, about Ma.

'Have you ever been on a tram?' she asked.

'No, I have not. But I have seen pictures. Grandma talked to me about them. Tell me, Rebecca – what is they like? How does they work?'

She described the wires that stretched overhead like filaments of a spider's web, the whirring and clanking, and how she and Ma had seen a strange white tram in the middle of the night, and they'd both thought it was a ghost.

'A ghost? Not really?'

'No.' She laughed. 'It was a special tram for cleaning the rails.'

Willem shook her hand. 'Tell me more, Rebecca. One day, maybe . . . I . . .'

Rifke knew he was thinking about his dream of becoming an engineer. It would be lovely to show him Johannesburg. Perhaps after he'd brought her back to

Ma. She ran through a scene of Willem moving in his knock-kneed way across the living room, his arm out-stretched to shake Ma's hand, and Ma reaching for his hand and holding it in both of hers, tears pouring down her fat cheeks, blessing him for looking after her precious daughter.

'Have you ever seen a movie?' Rifke asked.

He shook his head. 'But I knows about them from the newspapers Moeder's sister sends.'

Rifke told him about going to the Alhambra cinema, and how she and Ma lifted their feet off the floor to avoid the mice. They both laughed about that. She didn't tell him how Ma grunted whenever the story took an unex-pected turn, when the villain did something evil and then again when he or she was brought to justice. And how that had always made her so annoyed she'd wanted to do something, anything, to make her stop.

'And your father – is he fighting in the War?' Willem asked.

Rifke stiffened. 'No . . . maybe . . . I don't know,' she said after a few moments. 'I don't know if he is even alive.' She looked down. 'I used to dream – not very long ago – that he was a hero, like a film star. I used to dream that he would rescue me from . . . from my mother.' She looked up, caught Willem's eye in the windscreen's reflection. 'He went away when I was very small. Ma – nobody . . . spoke of him again. I think – I think he wasn't a good man. He was a drunkard. Maybe violent also.'

Willem shook his head.

'Willem,' Rifke said, 'you know how sometimes you think a thing, you believe it so much, so fiercely, that you just can't – won't – open your mind to it not being so?' She took a deep breath. 'Oh, I'm sorry, I'm not explaining it very well. But, I – I think I am beginning to understand some things about my mother's life.' Rifke began to tremble, and tears brimmed in her eyes. 'To understand how difficult everything has been – is – for her.' She swallowed. 'Willem, she has always tried to protect me – not telling me about my father, that was part of it. I didn't think she loved me, Willem – and I thought I hated her, but . . . but . . .' A sob broke free, and pulling her hand away from Willem's she bent over and buried her face in her palms.

'Rebecca,' Willem murmured. He slowed the truck to a halt beside the road and turned towards her. She felt the heat coming off his body. He touched her hair, and his hands were trembling. Slowly he put his arms around her, drew her in and stroked her back. He spoke soft words she couldn't quite hear as she leaned against him. His chest was warm beneath her cheek. She closed her eyes and heard her heart beat in time with his, breathing in his smell of engine oil.

A howl coming from somewhere in the bush startled both of them.

'We must keep driving,' Willem said.

When he took his arms away, the rush of sudden cold brought goose pimples to Rifke's skin. She tugged the blanket around herself.

'Sleep a bit, Rebecca.' Willem smiled at her. He started the engine, and, curling up on the seat, Rifke found her eyes closing again.

Chapter Forty-Four

'No, son. That is all I have. The War, you see.'

The truck had stopped. Rifke rubbed her eyes. Willem
had opened the car window and was talking to someone.
It was pitch dark and they were parked in front of a
couple of dilapidated buildings – a boarded-up shop and
an old garage with a petrol pump. A weak light came from
a window above the garage. A woman, ranks of curlers in
her hair, leaned out.

'Tell him he can take it or leave it, Jack!' The red spot
of her lit cigarette stabbed the air. 'Waking us up at this
hour – what a bladdy cheek!' Her voice rang out in the
silent night air.

'Yes, sir,' Willem said. '*Ek verstaan* – I understand. Do
you know if there is somewhere else along here that
maybe has some more petrol? It is just, I – we – really
need to get to Johannesburg.'

The man sucked in his breath and leaned on the open
window of the truck. He peered in, his fingers rasping at
his stubbly face. 'No one else around here with petrol,
son. And as I said, not enough in the pump to get you to
Jo'burg. Don't know when the next delivery will be.'

'Jack!' the woman yelled from above.

'We'll take what you have,' Willem said quickly. 'How much – Is there enough to get us to . . . Kimberley?'

'*Ja* – plenty for Kimberley. Maybe a bit further.'

Willem turned to Rifke with his eyebrows raised in question. 'Would Kimberley be all right?'

Rifke nodded. Kimberley was almost as good as Johannesburg. Uncle Ber could drive her home. '*Ja, ja*. Kimberley's fine. Thank you.'

The man stared at her for a second, then moved over to the rear of the truck. Rifke heard him unscrewing the petrol cap. Fumes filled the air, drifting into the cabin. She shivered. But it was going to be all right.

Willem climbed down from the truck and reached into the cabin for the hessian sack. He rummaged inside and pulled out a leather folder. There was a rustle and jingle; he gathered money into one hand. As he moved away from the truck, something fluttered off the seat. A gust of night air brought it to Rifke's feet. She bent to pick it up. 'Dearest Willem . . .' The words caught her eye. It was a letter. The signature drew her in. 'Your ever-loving Grandma Cecily'. Rifke held the letter in her hands and turned her head away.

Outside, Willem was negotiating the cost of the petrol with the man. Their voices were raised.

She shouldn't read it.

And yet she couldn't stop herself.

Before she set her eyes free on the looped writing, she knew what it would say. 'It is not much, my darling grandson, but it is a start. Aim high, Willem. Do not let Driemieliesfontein become your prison . . .'

Rifke thrust the letter away from her. It was his inheritance. More than that – it was his hope, his dream. And he was spending it on petrol to get her home. She flipped the handle on the truck door and leaped out.

'No, Willem!' she shouted.

The man was already walking away. The coins tumbling into his pocket, the wad of notes tucked into his waistband.

'That's the last time you get up in the night to sell petrol, Jack!' the woman shrieked from upstairs. 'And you two – clear off right now! Go on, get moving!'

Rifke darted to Willem's side. 'Willem, you shouldn't have . . .' she started to say. He took her arm and led her to the passenger side of the truck. His hands were empty. He'd handed over every penny.

'Let's go, Rebecca.' His voice was soft; he spoke quickly. 'Let's get out of here.' He looked older, and tired. It was too late to do anything about the money now. Rifke would tell Uncle Ber. He'd reimburse Willem.

Chapter Forty-Five

Dawn began with an orange stripe at the base of the windscreen. They'd stopped to drink some of the coffee Willem had brought. It was cold and poisonous-tasting, but it jolted them awake almost instantly. The sandwiches were long gone. They shared the last apple. Willem flung the core out of the window.

'Twenty-five miles to Kimberley. Isn't that what the last sign said, Rebecca?'

A ripple of something – excitement at seeing Uncle Ber and Aunty, Mirele, Farieda and Alfred, nerves also – made Rifke tremble. Something else too that cut through her. She looked across at Willem. He was sweeping his hair off his forehead, the angles of his face lit by the rising sun. How could she say goodbye to him?

He must have felt her gaze, because he turned. He tried to say something, then stopped himself and even in the dusty light she could see that he'd coloured. Somewhere in a field nearby a rooster crowed. The truck's engine tapped. Rifke looked down, then up again. Willem cleared his throat. Rifke spotted a bit of apple stuck to his cheek. She laughed and reached to flick it away. He leaned towards her at exactly that moment, and suddenly their faces were up close.

Rifke's heart leaped. Willem bumped her nose with his. She put up her hand and knocked his glasses askew. When their lips met, he tasted of apple and coffee and berry jam – and she knew she must too. She put her arms around his neck and held on to him, and when he tightened his grasp around her back, she didn't want him ever to let go.

It was the first time a boy had kissed her; and she knew that, apart from Izula, Willem hadn't met a girl her age before, let alone kissed one. Neither spoke. Rifke felt words stick in her throat like hard crusts. The nearer they got to Kimberley, the further she was going from Willem.

Widening bands of orange brightened the inside of the truck cabin.

'Rebecca . . .' Willem whispered.

She knew. It was time to go. They let go of each other, but Willem's glasses had become tangled in her hair and in his. They both laughed as Rifke disentangled them, but there were tears in Willem's eyes.

Chapter Forty-Six

They came upon Kimberley very suddenly. One minute there was desert, a sprinkling of sandy farms, the next the bleached sign '*Welkom na Kimberley* – Welcome to Kimberley,' and low-built shops and houses. They stopped a couple of times to ask the way.

Willem drove slowly, obviously unused to steering down streets. He looked around him wide-eyed. Rifke could hardly sit still. A nerve in her leg started jumping. She clamped her hand around it to stop it. Her teeth chattered, but she wasn't cold. She wanted him to speed up. She wanted him to slow down.

They turned a corner, and they were there. Aunty and Uncle's road. It was all so familiar, as if it were still that morning only one month before. There were the black or coloured servants watering the gardens, cleaning the *stoeps*, walking the dogs.

'Oh, Willem! We're in the right road. There! There! That one's Uncle and Aunty's house.'

The house was almost as it had been. But not quite. Uncle Ber's car was in the drive, but it didn't have its usual duck's neck gleam. The flowers looked dry and bedraggled. The grass was yellow. Something was wrong.

Willem stopped the truck. Rifke flung the door open and leaped out.

'Wait, Rebecca – don't forget this!' He leaned across and passed the blue canvas bag to her.

'Thanks. But you are coming in with me – aren't you?'

'No . . . er . . . I will just . . . there is something I must do to the engine.'

'Can't it wait? I really want you to meet my aunt and uncle and my sister, and Farieda and Alfred. I know they'll want to say thank you to you. And you must have a rest and something to drink.' She looked up at him. 'And you know what – you could come with us to Johannesburg!'

He smiled and mumbled something, and picked at a loose thread in his shirt.

She could see he felt shy. She'd feel the same. 'Oh, all right. See to the engine. But please, Willem – you have to come in as soon as you've sorted it out.'

When she reached the front door, she turned. He was standing beside the truck, his door open, one foot on the running board. A breeze ruffled his hair, and he raised his hand.

She rang the bell. The front door opened. Alfred stood there, the brass tray under his arm. He staggered backwards and let out a hoarse roar, the false teeth clattering in his mouth. Then he tried to shut the door against her.

'Alfred!' Rifke pushed her foot into the closing gap. 'It's me. It's Rifke.'

He put out a slow finger that quivered with fear and touched her hair. Rifke laughed. 'It's me, it's really me, Alfred. I'm not a ghost. I'm alive!'

He made a high-pitched keening sound. It brought Atticus careering into the entrance hall, barking his head off, and Aunty scuttling behind him. She stopped in her tracks and clapped her hands to the top of her head. Her mouth made up-and-down movements, but no sound came out. Rifke ran to her and flung her arms around her. There was less of her than usual; her back was knobbly.

'Ber! Come here, Ber!' Aunty finally managed to scream.

'What is it? What's happened?' Uncle came bustling in, followed by Mirele, who let out a shriek.

They all surrounded her, Aunty touching her hair, her face, her arms to make sure she was real. Atticus barked and snuffled at her shoes. She found herself being swept off to the kitchen, Aunty and Uncle and Mirele all shouting.

'Where've you been, Rifke? Where did you go?'

'Somebody take the dog outside!'

'Why didn't you telephone, let us know where you were?'

'Are you all right? How did you get here?'

'Look your legs are cut! Rifkele, Rifkele, what happened to you?'

Rifke looked around, dazed now by the shock of actually being there. The kitchen felt different. Emptied out. Cold somehow.

'Where's Farieda?' Rifke asked, interrupting them.

'She left,' Uncle Ber said. Rifke noticed the middle button of his jacket was hanging by a thread. He looked rumpled. 'Ten days after you disappeared, she packed her stuff.' He shrugged. 'We don't know where she is.'

Alfred was standing by the door, gripping the tray with one hand and Atticus's collar with the other. 'She doesn't want to stay here when you are not coming back,' he said, and he looked so sad Rifke went over to hug him. He patted her head absently.

'Mirele, put on please the kettle to boil. Rifkele, you'll have a little tea. Sit, sit,' Aunty said, patting a chair.

'Thank you, Aunty, but first I must telephone Ma. Please, Uncle Ber, will you take me to Johannesburg?'

Aunty and Uncle looked at each other. Mirele started to speak, but Aunty put a hand on her arm and silenced her.

Rifke's heart began to hammer against her chest. 'What? Something's wrong – I knew it! Something's happened to Ma!' She grabbed Uncle's sleeve. 'Tell me! Tell me what's happened!'

Uncle Ber put up both his small wide hands. 'Rifke, Rifkele – I will tell you. Toiba – your mother – is not in Johannesburg.' He turned to look into her eyes with his

272

soft grey ones. 'When you did not return, she had some sort of collapse . . .'

Rifke drew breath sharply. 'Collapse? Wh-what kind of collapse? Is – is she . . . ?'

Uncle took her hand. 'We don't know what happened. The Leibowitzes found her. They worried when she didn't bang on the wall as usual.'

'B–but, Uncle – is she . . . is she – has she –' Rifke whispered the last word – 'died?'

Aunty frowned. She tutted at Uncle Ber and shook her head, and loose skin at her neck that Rifke had never seen before waggled a bit. She moved to Rifke's side and put her arm around her.

'Rifke,' Aunty kissed her forehead. One of her tears landed on Rifke's cheek. 'Your mother – she has not passed away. For a couple of weeks she stayed in hospital. Ber and me – when the doctors said we could, we fetched her here. Three days past,' Aunty said.

'She's here? Quick – where is she? I must see her!' Rifke pulled away and made for the door.

'Wait, Rifke!' Mirele stood in front of her. 'Please – Ma's – she's not the same as you remember her. She's hardly eating, and the doctors have given her all sorts of medicine. To sedate her. She sleeps most of the time.' She tried to lead Rifke to the kitchen table.

'No, Mirele! What are you telling me?' Rifke shouted, flinging Mirele aside. 'You can't stop me. I've got to see her!' Her body was trembling. She felt as though all her blood had drained away. 'Please, Aunty – let me go to her.'

Aunty took a deep breath and looked questioningly at Uncle Ber and Mirele. It was strange how they all looked so much smaller. Even Mirele. 'Yes. Come. Come, Rifke. Let us go to her,' Aunty said. 'She is in the front bedroom. When she is awake, she likes to look out at the street.'

Rifke barely heard her. She was already through the door.

'Wait! Careful. Careful, Rifke!' Aunty warned from behind her.

Out in the passage, Rifke darted to the front bedroom, normally Aunty and Uncle's room. She stood outside the door for a second, her hand on the handle, trying to calm her breathing. From the street she heard people chatting as they walked by, a truck's engine coughing and retching to life.

A truck? Willem's truck?

A sound came from inside the bedroom. No more than a sigh. Ma.

Rifke hesitated for a fraction of a second, then opened the door. The curtains were drawn. It smelt of the inside of Ma's medicine case. It took Rifke's eyes a moment to adjust to the grainy light. She tiptoed across the room.

The tiny doll lying so still on her side in the bed had long thin hair that straggled behind her on the pillow. The final three or four inches were dark, the rest a

streaky grey. Her nose was a sharp beak and her cheek-bone pressed through the skin like a knuckle.

'Ma?' Rifke whispered. The hand lying on the bed-cover felt as light as a chicken's claw, and just as scaly and dry. 'Ma,' Rifke said again.

There was no response. Just the slow breathing, deepening now and then into the sigh Rifke had heard through the door. Rifke rested her hand on Ma's forehead. Then drawn by a powerful impulse she moved towards the window and pulled back the curtain.

The truck was gone.

A breeze riffled through the trees, the desiccated bushes, the feathers in the hat of a woman walking by and the leaves lying in the space once filled by Willem's pick-up truck. He might never have existed.

And Rifke had known. She'd known when he held her so tightly, when she'd seen the tears in his eyes, and in that moment when she'd turned to look at him and he'd raised his hand. She'd known that he would go.

Her heart swelled with an ache so heavy she wrapped her arms around herself as if to support it and sank on to the corner of Ma's bed.

He was gone.

Wherever in the *bundu* it was – and she would probably never be able to find out – Driemieliesfontein was another world. Her eyes brimmed with tears. 'Willem . . . Willem,' she whispered. But she knew, as he did, that he was needed there. His mother depended on him, and so did Hendrik and Piet. Sibu too. Rifke closed her eyes.

Travel safely, Willem, she thought. Come back one day.

She opened her eyes and put her hands out. The grease smears from his fingers had come off on to hers. Smiling through her tears, she put them to her cheek.

There was a movement from the pillows. Rifke leaped to the bedside as Ma moved her head with creaking slowness.

'Ma! It's me, Ma. It's Rifke. I'm back!'

Ma's eyelids fluttered, veined and translucent.

'Ma!' Rifke put her face near to Ma's and breathed in Ma's smell of medicine and face powder. She climbed on to the bed and curled against Ma's back and bent legs. Rested her cheek against Ma's nape.

'Rifke?' Ma's voice, at first a tight, dry sound, became hoarse with repetition – 'Rifke?' – and then as she reached behind her to pat at Rifke's shoulder, it became stronger, and lifted with joy.

Gaby Halberstam

BLUE SKY FREEDOM

'You just don't get it, do you? These people are ruthless. I don't care what they do to me, but no one else must be harmed.'

Victoria's childhood friend Maswe has been badly beaten up and he needs somewhere to hide. Victoria agrees to help him, but soon the police are asking questions and searching her house. What has Maswe done?

As Victoria's feelings for Maswe deepen she makes a dangerous journey to deliver a vital message, risking her own life to keep his safe. But apartheid is tightening its brutal grip on the country and Maswe doesn't want to hide forever . . .

A story of love, loss and courage set against the backdrop of apartheid-torn South Africa.

Shortlisted for the Waterstone's Children's Book Prize

A selected list of titles available from Macmillan Children's Books

The prices shown below are correct at the time of going to press. However, Macmillan Publishers reserves the right to show new retail prices on covers, which may differ from those previously advertised.

All Pan Macmillan titles can be ordered from our website, www.panmacmillan.com, or from your local bookshop and are also available by post from:

Bookpost, PO Box 29, Douglas, Isle of Man IM99 1BQ

Credit cards accepted. For details:
Telephone: 01624 677237
Fax: 01624 670923
Email: bookshop@enterprise.net
www.bookpost.co.uk

Free postage and packing in the United Kingdom